Wha

DEATH OF THE YELLOW SWAN:

I'm openly, unabashedly a fan of Steven Roth. I read everything he writes, usually start to finish in one sitting so that I can immerse myself completely in whatever scenario he presents. This is a particularly interesting series. I'm a huge fan of Art Deco, Film Noir, and historical accuracy. ALL of these are present in this book, with the noir setting of the entire novel taking me somewhere I want to go. I decided to try reading this in pieces, which resulted in my missing my subway stop on several days. So, I have to just suck it up, and slurp the book down, and admit I have a problem. I'm already looking forward to whatever Mr. Roth has in store for us for the next book. Read and enjoy. On a side note, I'm dumbfounded that his books are not being made into movies. The plots warrant it.....all of them.

—PP

What people are saying about

DEATH IN THE FLOWERY KINGDOM:

I am a dyed-in-the-wool aficionado of author Steven M. Roth and his brilliant detective novels. This time, Steve Roth turned the tables on me by taking his readers to Shanghai, China, year 1935, via ***DEATH IN THE FLOWERY KINGDOM***. We are introduced to a fascinating old school, Chinese Inspector Detective Sun-Jin. The reader is immersed in several clashing Chinese cultures.

I am impressed with author Steven Roth's meticulous

research and well-crafted descriptions. I could place myself on the streets of Shanghai as the author forms engrossing word pictures in his description of Shanghai in the 1930s. Mr. Roth's clear writing style helps the reader negotiate the twists and turns of the compelling plots and sub-plots of every one of his brilliant detective novels.

—WJC

What people are saying about
NO PLACE TO HIDE:

NO PLACE TO HIDE is a tense, beautifully sculpted novel that blends international politics, the military, and of course crime. . . .When an author is able to strike a chord of fear with the opening lines, the reader can be assured the designated genre of 'suspense novel' is correct. Steve does this with direct ease. . . . . And [after this opening], we're off and running and that [fast, tense] pace is sustained throughout this fine book. . . .Reading this second installment of the Trace Austin series develops a need to read the entire series — and that is a solid sign that Steven M. Roth is a novelist of significance.

—Grady Harp, AMAZON HALL OF
FAME TOP 50 REVIEWER

What people are saying about
NO SAFE PLACE:

Steven Roth has written a terrifyingly real bioweapon suspense novel. He has the chops to keep a reader turning pages and anxious about what comes next. *No Safe Place* alerts us to what the government has done and may still be doing to an unsuspecting and unconcerned public. Highly recommended.

—Charlie Stella
Author of *TOMMY RED* and eight other crime novels

What people are saying about
MANDARIN YELLOW

A splendidly told and sophisticated tale by a first-time novelist. The multi-layered murder mystery not only remains engaging throughout, but also offers the reader a superb primer on Chinese culture and history, particularly post-World War II history.

If you're a mystery fan, you shouldn't miss this novel that features a Parker Duofold (the eponymous Mandarin Yellow). This is prime mystery: well plotted and compellingly written. Roth weaves a taut storyline, paces it perfectly, and wraps it in twists and turns that make no sense until you get to the end (when everything clicks perfectly into place). Along the way, he slips in all the clues you need to solve the mystery right along with hero Socrates Cheng.

What people are saying about
THE MOURNING WOMAN:

There are never enough five star mysteries out there for a dedicated reader like myself. Steven Roth has now written another in his Socrates Cheng private investigator series called, "The

Mourning Woman." His first was, "Mandarin Yellow," which I thought outstanding. Both have fascinating, complicated plots involving a mix of Chinese and Greek cultures. Roth's extensive credentials in the study of these groups has provided him with a unique perspective that fits perfectly with the genre of intrigue, historical vendetta, and motives unlikely to be uncovered easily by a typical American detective.

The Mourning Woman, the second in the series of Socrates Cheng mystery novels, is an intelligent and engrossing murder mystery that is stylish, well-crafted, and every bit as satisfying as Steven M. Roth's debut Cheng mystery, Mandarin Yellow. Roth is a great storyteller. I look forward to the third installment of the series.

What people are saying about
THE COUNTERFEIT TWIN

Compelling, fast moving, suspenseful read. Iconic Confederate General Robert E. Lee's ancestry is central to this third novel in the Socrates Cheng series by rising author Steven M. Roth. You will be introduced to the world of Civil War reenactors, to a secretive Confederate museum that has been robbed of documents containing potentially explosive revelations, and to an accomplished, mysterious assassin for hire. All add up to a mystery that will keep you entertained and guessing until you have turned the final pages.

STEVEN M. ROTH

SLEEPING WITH THE TIGER

SLEEPING WITH THE TIGER

A 1941 SHANGHAI MURDER MYSTERY

STEVEN M. ROTH

BLACKSTONE PRESS
A CRIME BOOK IMPRINT

MYSTERY AND SUSPENSE/THRILLER NOVELS BY STEVEN M. ROTH

Socrates Cheng Mystery Series:
MANDARIN YELLOW
THE MOURNING WOMAN
THE COUNTERFEIT TWIN

Trace Austin Suspense/Thriller Series:
NO SAFE PLACE
NO PLACE TO HIDE

1930s-1940s Shanghai Mystery Series:
DEATH IN THE FLOWERY KINGDOM
DEATH OF THE YELLOW SWAN
SLEEPING WITH THE TIGER

Children's Mystery:
THE MYSTERY OF THE MISSING DONUT A
Mystery Introducing Owen Roth, Boy Detective

Written with Owen M. Roth
THE DOG WHO PLAYED CENTERFIELD:
A Dog & Baseball Story

SLEEPING WITH THE TIGER

Published by Blackstone Press, a Crime Book Imprint

Cover design by Streetlight Graphics, LLC

ISBN: 978-1-7328748-4-8

FIRST EDITION

Visit the author's website: www.StevenMRoth.com

Contact the author at: stevenmroth_author@comcast.net

For Dominica and Owen

"To serve the Emperor is like sleeping with a tiger."

Taoist Proverb

A NOTE ON SPELLING, DATES, ETC.

I have used the Wade-Giles romanization of Chinese proper names, provinces, rivers, creeks, towns, cities, and Chinese-language expressions throughout this novel because this was the transliteration method in use in the 1940s.

AUTHOR'S WARNING TO READERS

This novel, by current western standards, is not politically correct.

The story takes place in Shanghai in 1941. Many of the customs, statements, attitudes, and outlooks prevalent at that time not only might be alien to what we believe or accept in the twenty-first century, but also might be offensive to some people if portrayed in a novel set in the present-day.

Since SLEEPING WITH THE TIGER is a 1940s novel, I have tried to reflect the lives, language, and attitudes of the expatriates and Shanghainese people as they existed then, based on my research into then-contemporary English-language newspapers published in Shanghai, and also as reflected in many personal journals published after 1941. In doing so, I have deliberately not considered twenty-first century language, customs or sensibilities in writing this story. I use the slang and terminology, and try to reflect the attitudes, existing in Shanghai in the 1940s, even though these might jar current sensibilities.

If this might bother you, I suggest you not read this book.

PART ONE

CHAPTER 1

SOME JOBS ARE INHERENTLY DANGEROUS. Being a Shanghai municipal policeman or being a private investigator in Shanghai in 1941 are two such jobs.

Other jobs, such as being a comprador — an operations and finance manager for a taipan's business — typically are danger free.

Unless the taipan you serve happens to be Victor Sassoon.

Being the comprador for Sir Victor, as he prefers to be called, has been tantamount these past several years to volunteering for a death sentence.

This thought occurred to me while I was sitting in my office, located on Bubbling Well Road in Shanghai's International Settlement, reading the Chinese-language edition of this morning's *North-China Daily News*. The brief news story on page three of the paper caught my eye.

The story indicated that a little more than five weeks had passed since Victor Sassoon's comprador had been shot and killed as he left *Wing On* department store. I hadn't seen the original newspaper account of the murder, so this was fresh news to me.

Ayeeyah! — *Damn!* I thought, *That is not a job I would want, not for all the money, prestige, and influence that comes with it.*

This was the second of Sassoon's compradors to be murdered since 1937.

For the first time since 1935 when I was fired from my job as a Shanghai Municipal Police (SMP) inspector detective, I was glad I no longer was a cop and, therefore, not involved with the comprador's case. Every time I've touched something affecting Sir Victor, it's meant serious trouble for me.

I put down the newspaper and stood up to walk over to the electric hot plate where a cold, day-old pot of coffee awaited me. As I rinsed yesterday's coffee cup in the sink, my telephone rang.

I picked up the receiver and said, "Blue Dragon Detective Agency. Operative Ling Sun-jin here."

"Sun-jin, is that you, Old Boy?" the voice on the other end of the call said. "It's Chief Inspector Chapman here. I need to see you right away."

That stopped me cold.

Not only was I surprised the chief inspector was calling me — we haven't had any contact for almost four years — I was surprised he'd placed the call himself. Chapman had always insisted that his SMP cops follow the established customs relating to the privileges of rank and police decorum. When I worked for him, the chief inspector required that his adjutant-sergeant place his calls, then he reached out and took over the telephone when the other party came on the line. This departure from his usual routine — indeed, the fact he was calling me at all after all this time — made me suspicious. It could not, I believed, bode well for me.

Chapman had been my boss when I was an inspector detective with the SMP's Special Branch. He'd been my boss, that is, until six years ago when he fired me for insubordination.

After that, two years passed with no communication between us. Then, early in 1937, he pressured me into conducting a secret homicide investigation on behalf of the SMP. The case involved the murder of a controversial and popular Japanese nightclub singer known as the Yellow Swan. The combination of secrecy and the rules the chief inspector imposed on my conduct of the investigation almost made it impossible for me to solve the crime.

"Is there a problem, Chief Inspector?" I said.

"Get over here now. Then we'll see."

I put down the telephone and retrieved my suit jacket and tie from the wall-hook. I stepped into the water closet and stood in front of the mirror hanging on the wall.

I wanted to look professional, as well as prosperous, for the chief inspector. I slicked back my hair with Brilliantine pomade, tied my tie into a half-Windsor knot, and moved my face close to the mirror. I looked to see if I needed to touch up yesterday morning's shave. I didn't.

Then I left my office to go meet with Chief Inspector Chapman.

CHAPTER 2

Victor Sassoon was an Englishman by law although he'd been born just as his British parents passed through Naples, Italy, on their way to Iraq to join the rest of the Sassoon clan who had settled in Baghdad decades before.

In 1924, upon the death of his father in Baghdad, Victor became head of the family firm known as E. D. Sassoon & Company. For reasons he never publicly divulged, he soon thereafter relocated the business from Iraq to Bombay. The family's principle endeavor in India, as it had been in Iraq, was the exportation of opium to China.

Life in India eventually became tiresome for Victor, especially the repetitive hot, humid nights he was required to spend, because of his business and social standing, dressed in formal whites at excruciatingly-long dinner parties held by the British Viceroy.

Just before the global stock market crashed in 1929, and with ever-increasing numbers of nations enforcing laws against importing opium, Victor shut down that operation and decided to again move himself and his family's business to a new country. This time, based on visits he'd made over the years to the Sassoon offices in Hong Kong and Shanghai, he relocated the business to Shanghai. Once there, Victor bought land and built on it.

To do this, Victor transferred sixty lakhs of silver taels — the equivalent of about 39-million United States dollars — from Bombay to Shanghai. Once settled there, Victor's new business passion became the development of commercial real estate — hotels, office buildings, and luxury apartment buildings.

Sir Victor soon became an important real property developer in Shanghai, culminating in his construction in the International Settlement and in the French Concession of several Art Deco-style luxury hotels (such as the Cathay Hotel and the Metropole Hotel), modern office buildings (such as Sassoon House) and high-end, modern, residential rental complexes (such as Grosvenor House, Hamilton House, Embankment House, and the Broadway Mansions). Each of his buildings established a new standard of luxury and design for Shanghai.

While stock brokers leaped from skyscrapers in New York City, Sir Victor built new high-rise towers for various uses along the Bund — Shanghai's waterfront symbol of its obsession with business — where the city's most important bonded warehouses, banks, hotels, and clubs located themselves.

Eventually, Sir Victor's personal holdings, in addition to the luxury buildings he developed and operated on behalf of E. D. Sassoon & Company, ran the gamut from flower-seller girls brothels in the French Concession (popularly known as Frenchtown) section of the city, a brewery on Gordon Road, and the Jewish Day School on Seymour Road. In all, by 1941, Sir Victor owned, operated or leased-out under management contracts approximately 1,800 properties and businesses, large and small, throughout the city.

Although Sir Victor was one of Shanghai's richest and most powerful men, and even though he was a British expatriate citizen, he was not readily accepted by the city's ruling British class. He was not, for example, admitted as a member of the exclusive Shanghai Club, although he'd sought admittance on two occasions. The unstated, but well-known, reason for these two rejections was his religion. The Club did not admit Chinese, women, or Jews to membership.

Angered by this twice-repeated slight, Sir Victor acquired the mortgage held by the Hong Kong & Shanghai Bank against the Club's stately granite clubhouse building, located at No. 2, the Bund.

In one stroke, Sir Victor had become the Shanghai Club's banker, holding the Club's uncertain fate in his hands as part of his vast real estate portfolio. All this, he'd said to his comprador, as he laughed, at a time when many of the Club's members, for financial reasons resulting from the worldwide Depression, had given up their memberships or, if still members, were repeatedly late in the payment of their dues and bar bills, causing the Club's cash resources to ebb away, and making it difficult for the Club to avoid being in default of its monthly mortgage payments.

CHAPTER 3

After the chief inspector fired me six years ago, it was difficult to build my PI business from scratch. Some people, especially business people of all nationalities, were suspicious of me because I once had been a Special Branch policeman. They did not give me their trade. Other people, especially the British Round-Eyes, did not send business my way because they didn't believe that someone who was part Chinese could be trusted with their private or commercial affairs. The French did not give me business because I wasn't French.

Fortunately, I'd had some friends in the SMP who surreptitiously referred business to me, mostly from among people their colleagues had railroaded and arrested — people who need assistance in proving their innocence, proving that their only crime had been that they had not paid the required *squeeze* — *bribes* to the authorities. This business helped me, but, alone, it had not been enough to allow me to survive in a comfortable way.

To make it as a PI, particularly in that first year after I was fired, I mostly relied on the connections my elder brother — Sun-yu — had developed with several Celestial criminal triads — especially with Big-Eared Tu's powerful Green Gang.

Elder Brother — as I respectfully call him — owns a popular

nightclub in Frenchtown that is frequented by triad members. He has cultivated the friendship of these criminals because Elder Brother has delusions of himself one day becoming an important triad member.

Elder Brother and I have been close since early childhood, but this family kinship was enhanced when I was sixteen years old and he was twenty-one. At that time, our parents sent us to study at the Lutheran College in San Francisco in America. Fortunately, our British mother had always insisted we speak and read English, as well as Mandarin, at home. This helped us when we went to the English-speaking mission college. Because we both were lonely and had no Round-Eyes friends there, we leaned on each other, becoming even closer than we already had been in Shanghai.

When I graduated from college I considered becoming, among other things, a professor of English literature, a journalist, or an author. Instead, I become a SMP cop. Nevertheless, my love of language — English and Mandarin — has persisted, and I try to use the best vocabulary I can when speaking and writing. The only time I consciously deviate from that standard is when I am speaking with uneducated or under-educated people as part of my business. Then I speak *Hu* — the Shanghainese street dialect.

With Sun-yu's help, I have been able to assist triad members with investigations they need to have conducted, investigations they do not want anyone to know about. This is much like the work I did for Chief Inspector Chapman on the Yellow Swan murder case. Because I am discreet, I have become well-trusted among members of Shanghai's Chinese underworld, and that source has provided me with much business and, often, with critical information about other cases I'm working on.

Another source of business for me has been Shanghai's immigrant Jewish community. They, too, especially the Jewish merchants and tradesmen, always need the help of non-Jewish Shanghai citizens for business conducted by them outside their insular Hongkew community. For investigations, they generally turn to Chinese PIs since the Jewish community members and we Chinese have always felt a close bond based on our mutual respect for family, tradition, and education.

Gradually, as this diverse clientele has come to trust my discretion and my investigative abilities, my business has expanded so that I now find myself receiving more cases than I can easily handle. This is not a problem I regret having.

I left my office, hopped aboard the electric trolley as it screeched to slow down for me, and rode it to Chief Inspector Chapman's office.

I settled into a chair in front of the chief inspector's desk, and waited while he packed his pipe, took a long pull on the fired-up tobacco, and streamed out a cloud of blue, foul-smelling smoke.

"Good to see you again, Old Boy," he said, as he looked me over.

Said as if you hadn't fired me, as if I've merely been away on my own accord, perhaps on vacation from the SMP, I thought.

I nodded warily.

"*Zao an, sir — Good morning, sir,*" I said, speaking

Mandarin. The chief inspector prided himself on the seven or eight Mandarin words he understood. These were two of them. I switched to English.

"Good to see you too, sir."

I did not trust this situation.

"Well, Sun-jin, you've kept your end of the bargain and have been discreet in your business. That's good. I knew you would. I haven't had any reason to arrest you for flaunting your lack of a PI work license and pistol permit." He paused briefly. "Not yet, anyway. At least not that I know of."

Fankwei — Foreign devil! I thought. *Not yet? Not that you know of? Was that an implicit threat?*

"Yes, sir," I said, "I've kept my end of our bargain. Why are you even bringing that up?"

Chapman ignored my question.

"Did you know Sir Victor's comprador was shot and killed a little more than five weeks ago, right outside *Wing On* department store?" he said.

"*Ayeeyah!* Not until today, I didn't. I saw it mentioned in this morning's newspaper. It didn't give any details."

"Right," the chief inspector said. "That was intentional."

What's this have to do with me? I wondered.

"I need your help again, Sun-jin. This time in connection with the comprador's murder. Well . . . only indirectly in connection with that."

I said nothing. I stared into the chief inspector's eyes and waited for the ax to drop. *Was the chief inspector setting me up for another unacceptable assignment? Another secret, highly-conditioned Yellow Swan-type murder investigation?*

"I want you to run another investigation for me, one that will be carried on by you parallel to the comprador's murder investigation currently being conducted by the SMP. Much like before when you investigated the death of that popular Japanese nightclub singer.

"The difference this time is that this investigation will not be quite as secret as that other one. But you must conduct your investigation quietly, with great discretion, and out of the limelight, for reasons I'll explain."

I shook my head. "Secret? Again? Why, sir?" *I didn't like this.*

"You'll understand in a minute when I explain more to you. Sit back and relax. I think you'll find this case interesting."

"And if I don't agree to do it for you?"

"I wish you hadn't suggested that, Old Boy. Well, just like before. In that event, I'm afraid, I'll have to arrest you for conducting your business these past few years without the required PI license and pistol permit, even though you've kept your end of our previous agreement. It's nothing personal, you know, just business."

I sat quietly considering my response. The chief inspector puffed on his pipe and stared at me, waiting, I supposed, for my reluctant assent.

When I spoke, I shook my head and stood up to leave.

"*Ayeeyah!* No, Chief Inspector. I won't help you this time. You're wearing me down. You'll have to arrest me, if that's what you want. I'll just have to deal with that, then get on with my life."

I paused to give him time to back off, but he said nothing. He continued to puff on his pipe and stare at me.

I continued.

"I can't operate day-to-day not knowing if you're going to change your mind, undo our agreement, and arrest me if I refuse to do something new you want me to do. You might as well get it over with now, once and for all," I said.

As I turned away from him and faced the door, the chief inspector said, "Oh, sit down, Sun-jin. I knew you'd say that, but I had to find out, didn't I?" He laughed. "You can't blame me for trying."

I slowly turned back to face him, hesitated briefly, then returned to my chair. I didn't join him in his laughter.

"You can rest assured from now on I won't threaten you whenever I need your help. Not now that I know you won't be coerced. I give you my word." He paused. "Having said that, however, I do very much need your help."

"Yes, sir," I said. "I'm listening."

I was skeptical and did not want to commit to anything until I heard what the chief inspector's problem was, why he thought I could help him more than the SMP Special Branch could, and certainly not before he answered any questions I might have.

"As I said, the investigation, as such, does not have to be secret, but you must be discreet. I don't care if people know you're conducting an investigation, that's what private investigators do. But they cannot know you are doing it at my request, or that you are doing it for the SMP, or know what it is you're investigating."

"What's in it for me?" I said. I decided to use what little leverage I seemed to have at the moment to help my position.

"For one thing, an excellent fee, and perhaps, too, something intangible that will be even better for you in the long run."

Vague, but interesting, I thought.

"Okay, Chief Inspector, tell me what you have in mind. Then we'll see."

CHAPTER 4

BIG-EARED TU WAS THE UNDISPUTED crime boss of Shanghai (and of some other parts of China, too). He controlled the vast opium trade, the flower-seller girls prostitution business, all gambling clubs, the protection and extortion rackets, Shanghai's trade unions, and the French Concession police — having arranged for his Green Gang deputy, Pock-Marked Huang, to be Frenchtown's chief of police.

In addition to his criminal enterprises, and to advance the image of himself he liked to project, Tu also sat on the boards of directors of several legitimate banks, schools, fraternal organizations, and several charities. But at his core, Tu, who always spoke softly — especially when angry — was not the law-abiding, benign, elderly citizen of Shanghai he pretended to be. Nor was he the philanthropist he pretended to be — although he did dispense a great deal of cash in Shanghai in the form of *squeeze*, as one of his means of maintaining his authority.

In short, Big-Eared Tu was not a model citizen. He was a hard-core criminal, although a patriotic criminal.

Shanghai, in 1941, like much of China, was at war with the Japanese. The city has been involved in this undeclared conflict since August 14, 1937, the catastrophic day Shanghainese referred to as Bloody Saturday. It was the start of the Battle of Shanghai, as part of the larger Second Sino-Japanese War, which unofficially commenced in Peking on July 7, 1937.

There have been "three Chinas" within China since well before the start of the war with the Japanese.

Most of coastal China — including that part of Shanghai that lies outside the International Settlement and the French Concession, is occupied by Japan. That is one China.

Another China consists of that part known as Free (or Unoccupied) China. It is controlled, not by the Japanese, but by Chiang Kai-shek and his Kuomintang army and government (the KMT). Its people also refer to Free China as the Republic of China.

The third China is that part of the country that is controlled by the Chinese Communist Party (the . The CCP started in Shanghai, but was driven out of the city and into the countryside and mountains by the KMT, giving rise in 1934 to Mao's massive retreat from Chiang, known as the Long March.

The Battle of Shanghai was four years in the past when Big-Eared Tu received an important visitor at his home on Rue Wagner in Frenchtown. The visitor, General Dai Li, was the commanding officer of Chiang Kai-shek's secret intelligence service.

Tu welcomed his guest into his Great Room, an unlikely

stew of eastern Taoist and western Art Deco styles of art, scholars' artifacts, and furniture, including Persian pile rugs, Hunan lace doilies, a soft, European sofa, and several hard, unyielding, Chinese-made wooden chairs.

Tu's lucky crickets and caged songbirds fell silent when Tu and General Dai entered the Great Room.

As Tu guided his guest to the center of the room, Dai's gaze fell upon an exquisite, small, Tang Dynasty stone sculpture — *Head of a Crowned Bodhisattva* — sitting nearby on a pedestal.

Dai nodded his head toward the artifact, and said, "Your taste in fine art is exceptional, Master Tu."

Tu nodded, and gestured the general over to a silk pillow resting on the floor alongside a low, highly-polished boxwood table. The general stiffly lowered himself into a sitting position.

Tu lowered himself onto a pillow on the opposite side of the table. He faced the entrance door.

After the servant Tu had summoned brought their tea, then left, Tu slid his hand deep into the folds of his dark green Mandarin gown and withdrew a pack of *Hatamen*-brand cigarettes. He reached across the table, extending the pack toward Dai, and offered him a smoke. When the general hesitated, Tu said, "Take it."

Tu was not being polite. He was asserting his authority, in his home, over this powerful man.

They drank their tea and smoked their cigarettes. For a few minutes, neither man spoke. The ancient rite of tea-drinking prevailed above all else.

Following Taoist custom, and to save his host's face, when they finished their tea and cigarettes, the general broke the silence and spoke first.

"Master Tu," Dai said, "Thank you for welcoming me into

your home. I am here at the request of Generalissimo Chiang. He has urgent need for your help in his fight against the Communists and against the invading Dwarf Bandits."

Tu stared briefly at Dai, then shrugged slightly. "Explain yourself," he said.

CHAPTER 5

I SETTLED BACK INTO THE CHAIR in front of the chief inspector's desk, extracted a *Three Cats*-brand cigarette from the pack inside my jacket pocket, lit up, and prepared to listen to what Chapman had to say.

I wasn't convinced I wanted to help him, notwithstanding the possibility of a large fee and some other, intangible benefit he'd hinted at. My private investigation business was doing well, and I did not want to disrupt the flow of business, and possibly alienate my clients for the sake of one high-paying assignment. That would be short-sighted. But I would listen to what he had to say. I really had no other choice.

The chief inspector furtively glanced around his office as if he feared someone had snuck in through the closed door while we had been verbally jousting before.

He looked at me again. "What I am about to tell you is confidential. As I said, no one must know the subject matter of your investigation or who you're conducting it for. Agreed?"

I nodded. I hated obligating myself before I knew what I might be getting into, but the chief inspector left me no choice.

"As I mentioned, Sir Victor's comprador was murdered a little over four weeks ago, almost five full weeks ago, to be accurate. The SMP is still investigating that case, but has no leads yet."

I raised my eyebrows, surprised the case had not yet been solved or dropped altogether. The SMP had a well-deserved reputation for obtaining quick resolutions of crimes, through bribes or threats of arrest, or for dropping investigations altogether when the offense could not be quickly solved.

"In connection with that, as I said before, we held back an important piece of information."

I shrugged slightly. "Well, that's routine in a murder case, of course. When I was with the SMP, we often did that."

Chapman's face darkened. "There's nothing at all routine about this case. A comprador has been murdered. Sir Victor Sassoon's comprador. That's not routine."

Chapman's usual pale color soon returned. He leaned toward me. His voice and posture became conspiratorial. He spoke softly.

"What we didn't tell the press, and haven't publicly revealed, is that Sir Victor was with his comprador when the man was shot."

I couldn't believe my good fortune. Was Sassoon dead?

"Is Sir Victor also dead, sir? Murdered outside *Wing On*?"

The chief inspector shook his head. "Worse. Well, maybe not worse, but bad enough. Sir Victor was kidnapped when his comprador was shot."

I couldn't decide if this was good or bad *joss* — good or bad *luck* — for me. I had mixed feelings about it. On the one hand, I hoped Sassoon was miserable — as miserable as he caused my life to be by having me dismissed from the SMP. On the other hand, no one should have to go through the frightening experience of being abducted and held hostage.

"May I ask, sir? Is he still missing?"

The chief inspector slowly shook his head in apparent disgust at my seemingly naïve question.

"Of course he's still missing. Why do you think you're here, Sun-jin? What do you think we're talking about?"

"Has there been any contact from the kidnappers? A ransom demand? Some other demand?"

"Nothing. Just dead silence."

"And, I assume since I'm here, there's not been a body found in all this time that possibly could be Sir Victor's?" I immediately regretted asking this. I expected Chapman to explode again, but he did not.

"No body. Nothing but silence for more than four weeks, almost five."

Now that I knew the subject matter of our meeting, I was curious.

"Why do you think I can help, Chief Inspector? I assume the SMP has conducted a thorough investigation of both crimes."

"Yes and no. Yes, we've conducted a thorough investigation of the comprador's homicide, but no, we have not conducted a thorough investigation of Sassoon's kidnapping. We've kept that crime secret so the investigation has been limited. It's known to only a few people in SMP, and has not been completed. It still is in its early stages, and has been hampered by our need to conduct the investigation secretly. You should know all about that problem.

"To add to the pressure this case brings with it, we now also have to contend with Sir Victor's business partners who want him found before word of this gets out. They want the two crimes investigated and wrapped-up quickly and discreetly before anyone knows Sir Victor is missing.

"They're concerned that news of his kidnapping or, worse, news of his death, should it come to that, will cause the value of their real estate holdings and their stocks on the Shanghai Stock Exchange to collapse. They want to deal with that possibility before the information — whatever it turns out to be — becomes public knowledge."

I puffed my cigarette and nodded. *This could be a strange case.*

"If you'll take on this investigation for me, Sun-jin, Sir Victor's partners will guarantee you a large fee, however it turns out."

"And if I don't take it on, sir, then what?"

"I should add," he said, ignoring my question, "that if you rescue Sir Victor, if he's still alive, God willing, you will likely have his undying gratitude for the rest of your life, rather than his antagonism, as you have now."

I thought about that. It sounded plausible. But based on my previous experience with the chief inspector's secret investigations, I remained skeptical and silently defensive. I knew that as soon as I said I would conduct the investigation, if I said that, the chief inspector would impose additional conditions on my probe, just as he did the last time with the Yellow Swan investigation.

I had to established some rules between us before I agreed to anything.

"If I agree, sir, what restrictions will you place on me this time?"

"Just a few. Discretion, of course, as I said. Also, some secrecy about the investigation for political and economic reasons. And, obviously, the need for speed in wrapping it up. No one has heard from Sir Victor for over four weeks. I have to assume that inquiries will soon be made by his competitors or by the press when they realize he's not been seen in Shanghai or publicly heard from for sometime."

"Will I have access this time to the SMP's reports and lab work, to all of its investigation materials relating to the comprador's homicide? This might give me a clue to the kidnapping."

"Of course you will. Why would I withhold those?" he said. "I want you to succeed in this investigation, not fail."

Why, indeed? I thought, as I again recalled the restrictions concerning Yellow Swan's murder investigation.

I had stalled long enough. I knew I had no choice in this matter. After all, I had to be able to operate my illicit PI business with the tacit cooperation of the chief inspector and, now, with the cooperation of the taipan, if he still was alive.

"All right, sir," I said. "I'll do it."

CHAPTER 6

I LEFT THE CHIEF INSPECTOR'S OFFICE not sure if I was happy with, unhappy with, or just wary of the chief inspector's assignment. I definitely was suspicious of his unstated (and, as yet, undefined) motive for causing me to run a kidnapping investigation parallel to the SMP's homicide investigation. I tried to convince myself that I'd had no choice but to accept this. Perhaps I was right to do so, but maybe not.

I caught the electric streetcar to Jinkee Road in the French Concession. This was where my girlfriend, Wu Mei-hua, lived. I wanted to tell her about my meeting with Chapman.

The French Concession, which is considered part of France, not part of China or Shanghai, follows different operating rules than do Great Britain's International Settlement or the several Shanghai districts occupied by the Chinese, White Russians, and Japanese. The French Concession is ruled by a council appointed from France, not governed by a locally elected council.

Frenchtown, with its wide boulevards and tree-lined streets is an ideal place to live, a comfortable alternative to Chapei, where I live, or to the commercial-heavy International

Settlement. Its homes run west from Avenue du Roi Albert to where it intersects with Avenue Joffre. This quiet, residential environment suits Mei-hua very well, although, because of her values, it should not.

For all its beauty, the French Concession has its dark side. Since most of the foreign trade of Shanghai is carried on in the International Settlement, the French Concession finds it difficult to raise revenue for its municipal operations. To counter this, Frenchtown depends on income derived from operating licenses issued by it to opium dens, flower-seller girls' houses, and gambling emporiums.

Furthermore, because the French-based council governing Frenchtown has no interest in Chinese politics and lawlessness, the French Concession has become the favorite hideout for revolutionaries of all kinds and for fugitives from justice who cross into the French Concession to avoid Chinese politics and law. This territorial situation is aggravated by Frenchtown's proximity to the Chinese Old City, and by the rule that each concession's, and each district's, police power does not extend beyond its own borders.

This is, of course, a criminal's dream, a safe-haven for law breakers. A few streets here or a few miles there can put a criminal being pursued by the SMP or by the Japanese Municipal Police (the JMP) beyond the reach of one set of authorities and into the territory of another, with neither knowing nor caring much about what happened on the other side of its own border.

This parochial limitation is so strongly enforced by the policing authorities that Chinese police in Chapei have been known to shoot at SMP or JMP policemen, or to detain and arrest policemen, from across their borders, who wander into

Chapei in hot pursuit of a criminal or in the course of an investigation.

Mei-hua — *Beautiful Flower* in Mandarin — had taken my dog, *Bik* — *Jade* — home with her for the week. This was an arrangement we'd agreed to even though Mei-hua and I are in a thriving, year-long relationship. We both love Bik. Bik enjoys both of us. Since we are not married and therefore do not dwell together, we share my dog as if we are divorced, as if Bik is our only child we are made to share by the courts. Under this arrangement, I have Bik one week, Mei-hua the next. And, because we frequently spend nights together, we often both have custody of Bik at the same time. This arrangement seems to suit everyone, including, I think, Bik.

I played with Bik for a few minutes while I told Mei-hua about my new investigation. I did this — within the bounds of my promised discretion — so Mei-hua would understand why I would not be spending much time with her for the next week or two. I had cleared this disclosure with the chief inspector as a condition of my agreement to pursue his case.

I left Mei-hua's flat to go to my office. I did not want to wait for an available electric trolley to come along since available streetcars now ran infrequently under the Dwarf Bandit's new edict which required most streetcars to carry only members of the Dwarf Bandits' army — the Kwantung. Instead signaled to a passing coolie and rode his bouncing, bone-jarring rickshaw to my office.

I intended to close out the file of a case I'd just finished and to write the report to my client before starting Sassoon's case. I prefer things in my life to be organized and tidy — that's my Confucian upbringing.

I quickly finished the report. Now I turned my attention to the kidnapping of Sir Victor Sassoon. It was time for me to organize what little I knew about the case, to make a preliminary list of questions I might need to answer, and to figure out which of my usual, paid underworld informants I should talk to.

I also needed to think about kidnappings, in general. I had handled three or four kidnapping cases over the years, as a SMP Special Branch inspector detective, but it had been some time since the last one.

Kidnappings, I knew, seldom were random. Generally, the criminals had a specific target in mind for a specific reason. Usually for money, for ransom. But sometimes kidnapping occurred to achieve some other demand. I don't remember knowing about any kidnapping where the criminals didn't want something as a pre-condition to the safe return of the victim.

Typically, the family or business partners of the kidnapping victim receives a ransom or other type demand within twenty-four hours of the kidnapping. That did not occur here. Not even over the four or five weeks Sassoon had been missing. I didn't yet know what to make of that.

Because of this, I had no idea why Sir Victor's kidnapping might have occurred since money did not seem to be the motive. Perhaps, I thought, someone in Shanghai decided he'd become too powerful, and so had decided to put an end to that. But if that were the case, I would have expected his body to have turned up by now.

Even though I'd had my problems with Sir Victor, I hoped this was not the reason for his kidnapping. Because if it were, I then needed to be thinking about how to locate and rescue a man who likely already was dead. That is not what I wanted to do.

CHAPTER 7

In 1935, Avram Ben-David Reuben decided he'd had enough of his Breslau, Germany, homeland, with its ever-increasing and ever-vicious Nazi-inspired and enforced anti-Semitism. Avram decided he and his family would leave Germany forever.

Nineteen-thirty-five still was a time in Germany when Jews were encouraged to leave the country as part of solving the Jewish Problem. To do so, however — to receive the necessary permissions and the required travel papers — these hapless emigrants were required to turn in their passports (if they had passports) and their regional identity papers to the state, and to replace those documents with new papers that were stamped "J" in a large red letter on the first page. The new documents also were printed with a uniform middle name for each person — *Sarah* for the Jewish women and *Israel* for each man. They also were required to forfeit to the state all bank accounts and any other valuable assets they might possess that had not already been confiscated by local authorities.

Avram was prepared for this because he'd had friends who had left Germany in 1933 and 1934 under the same program.

Avram had paid attention to every detail his friends had been required to fulfill and to every obstacle they encountered.

To prepare for the day when he and his family would leave Germany, Avram had hidden money and jewels he intended to use for the trip. He also had a Gentile friend take possession of his rare-book collection, with the promise that his friend, at great risk to himself as one who aided Jews, would ship the books to him, in care of the local American Express office, once Avram and his family knew their final destination.

Avram retrieved the cache of money and jewels he'd systematically secreted away, packed up his family and a few of their remaining, portable possessions (specifically, Avram's valuable stamp collection), instructed his friend to ship the book collection to him in Shanghai, and, with his wife and three children in tow, began the long trek to Shanghai, the only city in the world that accepted the entry of immigrants who did not have passports or work visas.

The trip was long, slow, and punishing. It began with a train trip from Breslau to Hamburg, where Avram, his wife, his son, Eli, and Avram's two daughters would board a Nazi-controlled German ship bound for Genoa, Italy. From Italy, Avram and his family would sail to Shanghai.

The Breslau to Hamburg train was crammed with civilian passengers, members of Hitler's Brown Shirts, Wehrmacht soldiers, and, likely, too, members of the Gestapo, although Avram could not identify them in their civilian clothing.

As the train pulled away from the station in Breslau, Avram and his family huddled together in a corner at one end of a passenger-car. They were fearful of being noticed, singled out, and tormented because of their religion, even though the papers they carried demonstrated their right to be aboard the train. Eli, Avram's oldest child, closed his eyes and promptly fell into a furtive sleep.

When the train finally reached the station in Hamburg, a soldier boarded the car and shouted, "*Juden raus! — Jews out!*" Everyone else was told to remain on the train until a bus arrived to carry them to the wharf where they would board a ship that would take them to Genoa.

Avram quietly panicked. *What had gone wrong? Were there more indignities to suffer before they left Germany?*

Eli, hearing the soldier's shouts, abruptly woke from his nap. His eyes flew wide open. He was gripped by sudden and incapacitating terror. His hands shook. His face and neck reddened.

Not knowing what to expect, Avram and his family, along with the few other Jewish emigrants, filed off the train onto the station's platform. They huddled together in family groups with fearful anticipation. Soldiers forced them to line-up parallel to the train. A small cluster of black-clad SS officers and SS soldiers faced them.

When the Jewish passengers had properly assembled in a ragged line, one of the SS officers, flanked by several others, strode up and down the platform as if he were reviewing troops.

Distain painted his face. Disgust glinted in his eyes as if he were sullied by the mere act of being in the presence of

Germany's human garbage. He slapped a riding crop against his thigh as he walked back and forth along the line.

Periodically, he stopped in front of a wretched man, woman or child, their head bowed and eyes fixed firmly on their feet. He jabbed his riding crop into the chest of the unlucky person, who then was required to step forward and hand over their travel papers.

He performed this ritual eleven times before all the Jewish passengers were ordered to board a crowded, open-air dump truck that carried them to the wharf from where they would sail up the Elbe River, away from Hamburg, and onward to Italy.

Like all Jews emigrating to Shanghai, the Ben-David Reuben family traveled from Genoa by sea, carried by an Italian *Lloyd Trestino* ocean liner which charged the Ben-David Reubens — and the other 421-emigrant Jewish passengers — ten times the normal ticket price for the trip.

The voyage from Genoa to Shanghai lasted a full month. It was a trip that took Avram and his family through the Suez Canal, into the Indian Ocean, and, along the way, to the ports of Cairo, Aden, Bombay, Colombo, Manila, Singapore, and Hong Kong.

None of the seaports that welcomed the passenger liner allowed the Ben-David Reubens, or any of the other Jewish refugees aboard the ship, to disembark and enter the city when the ship temporarily tied-up to restock food and water, and to refuel. Gentile passengers were allowed to leave the ship and wander the port. All Jewish passengers were kept on board.

The day finally came when twenty-three year old Eli, his father, mother, and sisters stood on deck and watched as the liner slipped from the deep-blue China Sea and entered the Yangtse River. They stood by the railing as the vessel then chugged its way into the Yangtse's tributary, the muddy Whangpoo River. They almost were at Shanghai, at last.

The smell of the Whangpoo River, a blend of sewage, seaweed, and burned peat, was inescapable. Its landscape was dismal, flat, and uninviting. The ruins of small, colorless villages, and alarming mounds of bombed-out buildings, squatted along the shoreline in mute testimony to the Second Sino-Japanese War that had been raging for four years.

A motor-driven junk eventually chugged-up alongside their ship. The harbor pilot came on board. He would navigate the large vessel through the heavily trafficked Whangpoo, into her docking slip in Shanghai.

Most of the passengers, Eli's family included, stood along the railing as the liner approached the Bund. Gradually, the shore changed from huddles of commercial wharves to a long, wide, pleasant, tree-lined extension of the Public Gardens. Colorful flags whipped in the wind from several rooftops.

Eli's mother suddenly gasped, covered her mouth with her hand, and pointed at a large, gray, stone building in the distance along the Bund.

From its balcony flew the red-white-and-black flag of Hitler's Third Reich. The huge, hateful swastika fluttered mockingly in the breeze under the clear, blue sky.

"Have we come all this way just to be back in the hands of the Nazis?" Eli asked his father.

"That must be the German consulate," his father said, "because the Nazis do not control Shanghai."

No one spoke after that episode.

Dressed in their heavy European woolen travel clothes, Eli and his mother, father, and two younger sisters, all hot and uncomfortable from the oppressive heat and humidity, finally set foot on land once again when they stepped from the liner's gangplank onto Hongkew's passenger jetty. They were in Shanghai, at last, but alone with each other, having no friends or relatives there to pave their way toward assimilation. They were overjoyed, but wary. They had no idea what to expect.

Avram's first order of business was to find some place for his family to live. They spent their first three days and nights huddled together in a temporary barracks-like shelter provided by an international Jewish charity funded by Victor Sassoon. The living conditions were appalling, unlike anything Avram and his family had ever experienced. The shelter was overcrowded, filthy, and without indoor plumbing.

On the fourth day, Avram found a small flat to rent. He used some of the money he'd hidden from the Nazis to lease this small apartment.

Avram and his family gladly moved into this flat, which was above an enclosed commercial store-front stall that the landlord permitted Eli's father to use without additional charge. Avram set up shop there as a stationery dealer, a bookseller, and as a classic-postage-stamps vendor.

The flat was small, much less spacious and less convenient than had been their home in Breslau, but, as Avram reminded the family, "At least we now have a home we can live in with privacy and with minimum hygiene, unlike the fate of many of the Jewish immigrants who are forced to live in squalor."

The flat consisted of one room measuring 20 x 12 meters. It was moderately clean, especially when compared to the Wayside shelter they'd just left. It came with sparse, worn furnishings. The water closet was primitive, and reeked from mildew, but it was indoors and offered a real toilet having a pull chain. The flat's walls and floor were made from rough, raw, unpainted cement. There was one short, square bathtub in the room and one small sink. There was no hot water.

Downstairs, in his small, commercial stall, Eli's father, over the next weeks, stocked his store with left-over paper he bought from merchants in the International Settlement. He sold these remainders to professional letter writers — those educated, but unfortunate Chinese men who had dedicated their lives preparing to become civil servants, but who had failed their national examinations, thereby losing face. These individuals were finished as far as society and their shamed families were concerned. They could not return home to their villages. To support themselves, because no educated person in China ever engaged in any form of physical labor, these men remained in the city, set up tables alongside the street, and for a fee wrote letters on behalf of illiterate members of Shanghai's Chinese community.

Avram also sold books from his rare book collection, and he sold collectible postage stamps he'd brought with him from Breslau in the lining of a valise having a false bottom.

Stamps and books, not random sheets of writing paper, Eli would later say, enabled his family to survive in Shanghai in those early days.

Gradually, Avram's supply of stamps and books gave way to

empty shelves, with no chance for him to sufficiently replace his sold stock with new stamps and books. He could not continue that business. So Avram looked ahead. He decided people would always need money, especially small change. That would be the basis of his new business.

Avram turned his stationery store into a small-change shop, changing money for merchants and pedestrians, charging a reasonable fee for each transaction. He also loaned small sums of money to local merchants, upon their personal guarantees, with no collateral necessary, but at high interest rates. His business prospered and grew as the Jewish population in Shanghai prospered and grew.

CHAPTER 8

Big-Eared Tu listened carefully to what General Dai had come to ask him.

"As I said, Master Tu, China and the KMT need your help."

Tu nodded, but said nothing. After a half minute of silence passed, Tu ended the stalemate.

"*Kenong — No surprise*. All right, how much? My pockets are deep, General, but not without bottom. I already am subsidizing a large measure of Generalissimo Chiang's army."

Dai shook his head. "*Qing! — Please!* Not money, Master Tu. Not this time. As all Free China knows, your generosity in that regard has been, and continues to be, magnificent. We — the generalissimo and I, as is all China — are extremely grateful to you for the financial help you have given us."

Tu frowned, suspicious now of what the general might request. "What then, if not gold or silver?"

"We want you to enlarge your private network of spies, then direct their espionage not only against the Dwarf Bandits, but also against the Communist vermin who are taking advantage of our country's turmoil to strengthen themselves for after the war."

"Everywhere or only in Shanghai?" Tu said.

"For now, Shanghai only. Here, where you have the established basis for the most success already built into your organization."

CHAPTER 9

I FIRST MET MEI-HUA, THANKS TO Bik, just over four years ago. I had been shopping and had tied Bik's leash to a post in the lawn area outside the store set aside for dogs. When I returned from inside *Wing On* and went to retrieve Bik, Mei-hua was sitting on the grass petting her, and talking to Bik in rapid, high-pitched Mandarin as if Bik understood her.

Since then, notwithstanding her parents' objection to me because I'm not full-blooded Chinese and also because I'd been a policeman (not an honorable profession in the eyes of many Celestials), we've had a loving, ever-developing relationship. On its face, this is surprising since we have strikingly different personalities, although we do have some important interests in common, such as our love for, and study of, the difficult martial art known as *Shaolin*. But, at the core of our beings, Me-hua and I are very different.

Mei-hua is a revolutionary, in her heart and intellectually, always looking for ways to tear down and overturn our Celestial traditions and institutions. For many years, she was an active member of the CCP, with close ties to the Eighth Route Army. She had even followed Mao Tse-tung on the Long March north, away from Chiang's pursuing KMT, until she fell ill from fatigue and malnourishment. To regain her health, she'd had to drop out of the march. After a long period of convalescence at the rural home of a compliant peasant family, Mei-hua returned home to Shanghai to her KMT-colonel father and to her anti-Communist family.

I, on the other hand, am the product of a British mother and Chinese father who raised me as a strict Confucian, but also with some aspects of Taoism as part of my upbringing. This means that I believe in laws, rules, and obedience to higher authority — namely, to one's parents, to the state, and to all the state's bureaucrats. Accordingly, I happily adhere to our time-honored traditions. Unlike Mei-hua, I do not want to destroy our customs in order to create better ones. As a result of my beliefs, I sometimes take a full measure of teasing or scorn from Mei-hua. I've chosen to accept this.

On the surface, then, Mei-hua and I seem like oil and water, but we really are more like *Yin* and *Yang*, seamlessly complementing one another, the pieces of our personalities and experiences smoothly fitting together, while, at the same time, differing from one another, as opposites.

Mei-hua and I have discussed this many times over a glass of Tiger Wine, that foul-smelling drink we Chinese seem to adore for its harsh and corrosive properties. We have been able to find common ground and to plan our futures together. It is our hope that if we survive the current war with the Dwarf Bandits, we will marry and raise a family. In the meantime, Bik is our substitute child.

Bik woke us early this morning, just as the day's sun started to caress our window, by jumping around on my bed and licking our faces until, first, Mei-hua, then I, said, "*Ayeeyah dog!* —

Damn dog! Stop it, girl, we get the point. You want us to wake up. Now leave us alone. We're awake, thanks to you!"

Bik is not a dumb mutt. She still has her wild-dog instincts from the time we found one another near the Baby Drawer. But she knows when she's been bested, so she jumped off the bed and ran to the window. She put her front paws up on the windowsill and looked out at the street below. Her short tail wagged.

Mei-hua sat up, naked to her waist, and shook her head. "*Ayeeyah,* Sun-jin," she said, "you really must have a talk with your daughter. She must learn that visiting guests should not be disturbed when they sleep over for the night. She needs a basic lesson in lovers' hospitality."

I laughed and rubbed my eyes. The sun was now up and the sky its usual steel gray.

"Not me," I said. "I'm not talking to her about that. That's a mother's or an *Amah's* conversation to have with the daughter, not a father's duty.

We both laughed.

"She never listens to me anyway," I said. "If I talk to her, she will smile and wag her tail, but then go back and do whatever she wants to do. You try."

As if Bik knew she was the subject of our conversation, she turned her head back toward us and barked once. Then she looked out the window again and barked a second time. Then she barked again. This was not like her. Bik was a quiet dog.

Mei-hua wrapped the blanket around herself and left the bed. She walked to the window. There, she stroked Bik's head with one hand as they both gazed at the street below.

"Come look at this, Sun-jin," Mei-hua said. Her eyes remained fixed on the street as she called me over.

Below us, beginning to our right as far as I could see from our strained, fourth-floor angle of vision, then continuing directly below us, and going on again to the left of my flat, armed Dwarf-Bandit soldiers marched in a column four rows across. The soldiers' unending columns were interrupted occasionally by the presence of a tank or other armored vehicle, followed by more soldiers, then by another tank or vehicle, then more soldiers, as far as I could see in either direction.

These were our conquering occupiers, out strutting their power, as usual. Shanghai, in August 1937, had lost its round in the Second Sino-Japanese War. Those parts of the city — such as Chapei, where I live — that are not foreign treaty concessions (the International Settlement and the French Concession) — were now, four years after the Battle of Shanghai, occupied by the Kwantung army, and were vassals of our self-proclaimed protector, Japan.

CHAPTER 10

SIR VICTOR SASSOON WAS WITTY, idiosyncratic, mercurial, and privately cynical. He was quick to anger, saw personal slights where others might not, and wore his unending grudges like badges of honor. He also was powerful. He was one of the wealthiest and most influential Round-Eyes in the Settlement and the French Concession.

As his response to twice being denied membership in the prestigious and influential Shanghai Club demonstrated, Sir Victor was not a man to be trifled with or to be taken lightly.

On another occasion, when Sir Victor and his guests arrived late in the evening at a nightclub, and were turned away — ostensibly because the club was filled to capacity — Sir Victor soon thereafter purchased the vacant parcel of land across the street from the offending club, and built Shanghai's first air conditioned nightclub on the vacant site. He called the club, *Ciro's.*

Ciro's quickly became known for its plush accoutrements. It was most famous for its large ballroom with offered it patrons half-a-dozen elevated dining areas that were surrounded by gleaming metal railings. These railings, with the push of a button, sank into the flooring and disappeared, enabling the diners to step out onto the ballroom floor to dance.

Within three months of *Ciro's* opening, the offending nightclub across the street had been put out-of-business.

Sir Victor never married until late in life. After having seriously injured both legs in an airplane crash when he was a pilot during World War I, Sassoon carried the emotional and physical burdens of those injuries with him for the rest of his life. To walk, for example, he used one or, sometimes, two canes.

It did not take great insight for Sir Victor to decide that because of his infirmity, no woman he might want for his wife would also want him as her husband, other than for his wealth. So, until the very end of his life when he married his nurse, Sir Victor remained a resigned, dedicated bachelor and playboy, constantly surrounding himself with, and having affairs with, beautiful single and married women.

In a city known worldwide for its reinvention of individuals' histories and identities, for its frivolity and licentiousness, Sir Victor cut a large figure in Shanghai society. He openly indulged his voracious appetites for bizarre-themed costume parties he staged at his Cathay Hotel, for fine food and drink, and for his love of thoroughbred ponies he imported from the plains of Mongolia, and which he raced at the Shanghai Race Course.

CHAPTER 11

THE NEXT MORNING, I LEFT Mei-hua and Bik in my flat and headed for my office. On the way, I bought copies of the Chinese-language editions of the *North-China Daily News* and the *China Press*. I wanted to see if those newspapers said anything about Sassoon's absence from Shanghai. I doubted they would since it was supposed to be a secret, but I had to be sure. If they were silent, I then would go to the library to check recent back issues of those and other newspapers, going as far back as the day the kidnapping occurred.

As I expected, the newspapers had nothing in them that was helpful to me, so I left my office, crossed the street, and rode an electric trolley to a destination not far from No. 15, the Bund, the address of the public library. Because today was a rare day in Shanghai in which the sun was shining and the temperature was comfortable, I hopped off the trolley about ten blocks from the library and walked the distance to No. 15.

To walk along the Bund was to encounter Shanghai at its most vibrant. The street was alive with noise and movement. Horns honked, whistles blew as Sikh crossing-guards directed pedestrians to cross the boulevard, bells jingled, streetcar wheels screeched, peddlers of every kind loudly hawked their wares, and vehicles of every type — cars, buses, pushcarts, pony carriages, rickshaws, wheelbarrows, and motorcycles — streamed along the Bund in a mad rush.

I walked up the sixty steps to the library's entrance. The high doors were flanked by bronze lions. These lions are smaller than the two creatures that guard the entrance to the Hong Kong & Shanghai Bank building, but they serve the same purpose. The lions can bring you good *joss* if you properly respect them by touching one as you enter or leave the building they watch over.

Although normally I reject such superstition, on this occasion I followed the tradition and touched one of the lions as I entered the building. I decided I could use good *joss* as I embarked on my investigation.

I spent the next half-hour looking through newspapers that had been published since the date of Sassoon's kidnapping.

None of the papers mentioned Sassoon at all until I read the issues published two days ago, when the English-language edition of the *Shanghai Times*, and the Chinese-language edition of the *China Press*, printed short articles questioning, and then speculating about, why no one had seen or heard from Sassoon for many weeks.

Sassoon's habit, both stories pointed out, was to publicly announce his trips whenever he left the city for more than a day or two. He often would throw a lavish party the night before he left town so his name would appear in the society pages of the city's newspapers while he was away. It seems Sir Victor always wanted to keep his name in front of the public, even when he was not in Shanghai.

The Frenchtown newspaper, *Le Journal de Nuit*, also in the edition published two days ago, ran a small article on page two with a headline that asked, *Has Sir Victor left the city?* The sub-headline said, *No one knows or will say?* The story that followed offered nothing new to me.

The White Russian newspaper, *Shanghai Zaria — Shanghai Dawn* — also published in the French Concession, speculated that, *Perhaps Sir Victor has taken ill? No one has seen him in several weeks.*

And so it went among the four English-language newspapers, one English-language Russian newspaper, and nine Chinese-language Shanghai-based dailies I checked. Not one paper had any idea that a crime had been committed against Sir Victor, or, specifically, that he had been abducted. Not one of the papers tied Sir Victor's absence to the murder of his comprador or, if they did make the connection, not one newspaper was indiscreet enough to mention this.

So far, so good, I thought.

I touched the other lion on my way out of the building.

CHAPTER 12

JMP Inspector Detective Akio Harue stared briefly at the one suit of clothes he habitually wore to work each day during the summer months — his ill-fitting, tan, double-breasted linen suit. He wore this garment with a sword over his left hip and his 21mm Nambu Taisho Shiki pistol over his right hip, each attached to his belt.

Today, he left the suit hanging in the wardrobe. Instead, he pulled out and climbed into the special civilian-style uniform he'd recently been given by the commanding general of the Kwantung army now occupying most of Shanghai. He attached his sword and pistol to his belt.

Harue looked at himself in the mirror. His chest expanded. He seemed to himself to be taller now than his actual 1.4 meters — 5'4" — height.

He ran his palms over the front of his uniform's jacket, from his shoulders to his waist, carefully smoothing out all creases, visible and imagined.

This uniform meant much to him. The Kwantung general had issued it to him even though Harue was not a member of the military. It was an indication to him that the general had taken him seriously when he vowed to fully police the occupied districts on behalf of the Kwantung, and to report to the general all discovered, secret CCP members, secret KMT members, other dissidents of every stripe, and any other traitors — actual or potential — to the Emperor and to the righteous path his Emperor pursued against the cursed Chinese.

It now was four years since Japan won the brief Battle of Shanghai. In those four years, Harue had hoped to receive a specific, well-deserved assignment from the general, something that would allow him to attain recognition in the homeland of the superiority he inherently had over the resident Chinese of the city, and, of course, over the Round-Eyes from Britain, France, the rest of Europe, and from America. So far, his occasional hints to the general had fallen on indifferent ears.

Yet he continued to hope that one day he would receive some assignment from the general worthy of his unrecognized talent. He could not conceive what that assignment might be since he was not a soldier, but he stood ready to do his duty to fully carry out any task asked of him on behalf of the Emperor. he would strive to achieve his small part, whatever that part might be, in realizing the glorious goal of establishing the Greater East Asia Co-Prosperity Sphere in this wretched part of the world called China.

CHAPTER 13

AVRAM'S FAMILY WASN'T AMONG THE first Jewish families to re-settle in Shanghai. Jewish refugees had come there in small numbers for centuries. But with the rise of Nazi rule in Germany, and then in other European countries as that scourge swept its way across the Continent, Shanghai offered sanctuary to members of Europe's Jewish population at a time when western countries uniformly refused them admittance.

The Japanese government had a long memory, and it held Jewish immigrants coming to Shanghai in high regard, based on their recent history together.

In 1904 and 1905, when no country or financial institution would assist Japan in its dispute against Imperial Russia by financing its opposition to Russian expansion into Manchuria and Korea, it had been two small, Jewish-controlled banks in New York City that made loans to the Emperor. This enabled Japan to fight the Russo-Japanese War, and to drive the Russians from Manchuria and Korea. In return, the Japanese now welcomed Jewish refugees to Shanghai, and encouraged them to settle in Hongkew, a section of the city the Japanese had captured from China in 1937.

Hongkew was occupied by a dense, but poor, Japanese immigrant population. The invitation to the Jewish immigrants to settle there was, in part, Japan's effort to revitalize this rundown section of the city to benefit its Japanese citizens already living there.

The immigrant Jews, satisfied the Japanese were not anti-Semetic and would treat them well, accepted the offer and settled in Hongkew. The Jewish immigrants prospered there.

With the help of low interest-rate loans made to these refugees, loans offered by Victor Sassoon and by a few locally-based international Jewish relief organizations, many of these refugees opened businesses. The Jewish district within Hongkew soon boasted having tailor shops and watch-repair shops, as well as practicing doctors, lawyers, dentists, engineers, teachers, and other professionals. Schools at all levels of learning sprang up at a dizzying pace.

Gradually, the character of the so-called "Jewish section" of Hongkew changed to reflect its Jewish population, offering its European residents European-style restaurants, flower shops, jewelry stores, fur shops, dress shops, cafés, and household-goods stores.

The Jewish neighborhood evolved in ways the Japanese occupiers never could have imagined. Viennese men and women sat outdoors at cafes. They sipped coffee along Avenue Roi Albert, and savored the fragrance of freshly baked bread and pastries from nearby Austrian-style bakeries. There were Kosher butcher shops and German delicatessens. Shanghai's newspapers — specifically, the editions sold in Hongkew — were printed in Yiddish, Hebrew, German, and Polish. Abraham's Dry Goods store sold candles for Jewish holidays and for the Sabbath. The tango was danced nightly at Max Sperber's German-style *Silk Hat Club* cabaret located near Little Tokyo, the remaining Japanese section of Hongkew.

A unique Jewish community flourished. The neighborhood was widely referred to as Little Vienna.

CHAPTER 14

Big-Eared Tu gradually transformed his small army of spies, whose original purpose had been to keep Tu informed about rival triads, into a military-style espionage network unparalleled in Shanghai's recent turbulent history. He soon had 13,000 men and women under his control, snooping everywhere, and reporting back to him all manner of information about the Kwantung and the CCP.

But Tu's actions were not without consequence to him, not without potential, personally-directed danger against him. The Japanese were not blind to the potential military threat Tu represented to them. The Kwantung had its own coterie of secret agents at work in Shanghai, including some within Tu's own household.

The Kwantung's initial response to Tu's activities was to try to win him over to their side. They first attempted to bribe him, having heard that above all else, except for power, Tu craved gold. But Tu was too patriotic, too loyal to Chiang's Republic of China, and too wealthy to be bribed.

The Kwantung next tried to intimidate him, but Tu was too much the ruthless criminal to be intimidated by foreigners, and was too well-entrenched in Shanghai's underworld and its routine violence to blink at potential threats.

So the Kwantung decided to kill him.

One morning, a bomb exploded at Tu's home, damaging it beyond repair. His fifth wife was killed, his third wife badly disfigured. Tu was not frightened, but he also was not a fool. He knew when he was beaten, if only temporarily.

Tu sent a cadre of his trusted bodyguards, and his third and fourth wives, to Hong Kong, where they settled into a luxury suit at the Peninsula Hotel — a structure and operation matched in quality and splendor only by Victor Sassoon's Cathay Hotel in Shanghai.

Tu's second wife, who normally lived with Tu and his other wives, had been in Wuhan at the time of the explosion, visiting Tu's stepson, who boarded at the university there.

Tu's first wife, out of her mind from opium addiction, refused to leave Shanghai, even though Tu promised her an unending supply of the Brown Mud if she would join his other wives in Hong Kong. She refused to go, and soon thereafter died of causes related to her addiction.

Tu remained in Shanghai, in hiding, directing the growth and operations of his espionage network, which eventually expanded to 22,000 men and women, all answerable only to him. Tu had eyes and ears everywhere in Shanghai.

CHAPTER 15

Sir Cornell Franklin, chairman of the Settlement's Municipal Council, and current vice-chairman of the Shanghai Club, summoned Chief Inspector Chapman to meet with him at No. 2, the Bund.

The chief inspector was uneasy. He'd been to the Shanghai Club only twice before in all the many years he lived and worked in Shanghai. Neither of those visits had been social. On both occasions the chief inspector had been ordered to appear there. Neither of those visits had been a pleasant experience for him.

As Chapman stepped into the lobby of the three-story structure, he reflexively tilted his head up to gaze at the twelve-meter-high ceiling, painted sky-blue with puffy white clouds. He glanced across the room at the ornate doors of the twin, modern lifts that connected all floors, and at the long, curving white-marble staircase with its bright red carpet that ascended to the next level.

A tall Sikh, wearing a spotless white uniform and a bright orange turban, walked up to him and blocked his way beyond the immediate entrance.

"May I help you, sir?" The Sikh bowed his head slightly.

"I have an appointment with Lord Franklin. He's expecting me. My name is Chief Inspector Chapman."

"Of course, sir. I've been so advised. Please follow me."

The Sikh led Chapman to a small library having plush wall-to-wall, gray carpet. It was quietly organized with deep leather chairs and with several large tables that were randomly scattered about. The walls, except over the two fireplaces, were lined with floor-to-ceiling bookshelves, all filled with books. The ceiling lights and the amber table lamps were dimmed so no one could comfortably read, if they could read at all.

No one was in the room except Lord Franklin. He dismissed the Sikh with a curt nod and the statement, "Leave us." He turned his attention to Chapman.

"Be seated, Chief Inspector," Lord Franklin said. He took a sip of the sherry he'd been holding, then placed the glass on the small, round table next to his chair. He did not offer Chapman a drink.

"Are you satisfied with your job, Chief Inspector?" Franklin asked. He looked into Chapman's eyes, not breaking contact as he waited for the chief inspector's expected response.

Chapman briefly looked away, then quickly looked back again, fixing his gaze on Lord Franklin's left ear.

He squirmed in his seat and wondered if he was being threatened with losing his job, as he'd been on his prior visits to the Club, if he did not now obey some order from Lord Franklin.

"Of course, sir, I most definitely am. Most well satisfied. Just as always."

Franklin took another sip of his sherry, then placed the glass back on the table. He stared at the drink for a few seconds, then again looked up at the chief inspector. He narrowed his eyes.

"In that case, what I am about to instruct you to do shouldn't be a problem, Chief Inspector, not if you wish to keep your job. I have an order for you from the Council."

"Yes, sir." Chapman's back stiffened. This could not be good news.

"You will immediately cease all investigations involving the brief disappearance of that Hebrew, Victor Sassoon," Franklin said.

Chapman was puzzled. He rubbed his chin, and said, "Um . . . sir? Did I hear you correctly?"

"I assume you did."

"But, sir—"

"You heard me, Chief Inspector."

"May I ask why, sir?"

"No."

Franklin turned away from the chief inspector and lifted his drink to his lips. He did not turn back again to look at the chief inspector.

Their brief meeting was over.

CHAPTER 16

I WAS IN MY OFFICE ARRANGING to put a temporary hold on my active, pending cases so I could give top priority to Sassoon's case. This would be tricky. I did not want to offend my triad-criminal clientele by having them think I was neglecting them. I also did not want to offend my Jewish clientele by having them think I was treating them as if they were second class clients — as everyone else in Shanghai, except the Dwarf Bandits, treated them. I walked a delicate line here.

I decided I would devote my days to the chief inspector's investigation and a few hours each night to the other cases. At least I would try that to see if it was manageable.

Someone knocked at my door.

Ayeeyah! *Not more new business,* I thought. *I certainly can't handle that right now.* Then I realized what a foolish and ironic thought that was. I could use all the business I could get. Anytime. I would just have to figure out how to manage it all.

"Come," I said. "The door's unlocked."

I watched as the door slowly opened and, much to my surprise, Eli Ben-David Reuben walked in.

I first met Eli one year ago when I tracked down a Celestial merchant who had stolen a valuable postage stamp from Eli's father's commercial stall in Hongkew. As a result of that case, and the outcome I achieved for him, Eli's father, Avram, and I became friends. Since then, his father has referred much business to me from among members of his Jewish community, who do not trust, and do not want to deal with, the Settlement's SMP cops or with Round-Eyes private investigators.

I have run into Eli from time-to-time when I've had occasion to be in his father's neighborhood on other business. I always try to find time to visit Avram at his stall or apartment above, to drink some wine with him and his wife, to talk with him about our shared love of books and literature, and, most important, to trade gossip. On several of those occasions, I ran into Eli, and we exchanged brief greetings. I don't think we ever had a conversation.

"Hello, Mr. Ling," Eli said, as he walked toward my desk. He split his face with a wide smile and poked out his arm to shake hands with me.

"Sun-jin is fine, Eli. There's no need for us to be formal."

He nodded. "Thank you, Sun-jin."

I pointed toward the chair in front of my desk. "Have a seat."

I closed the open file sitting on my desk. "To what do I owe your visit? You're not in any trouble, I hope?"

Eli shook his head and laughed. "I'm always on the brink of trouble with my underground contacts and my political activities. But who isn't these days?" He paused, then said, "No, sir, not yet. No actual trouble for me so far." He rapped his knuckle twice on the top of my wooden desk, summoning good *joss*.

"Good." I nodded. "How can I help you? I know your first visit to my office isn't a social call."

"Correct, sir. I need your help. My father suggested I talk with you."

He paused, then sucked in a deep breath and slowly let it out as if his next statement portended terrible news. "I would like to become a private investigator, like you. Will you teach me?"

I never expected that.

"That's pretty ambitious," I said, "but pretty unlikely, too."

I watched Eli frown. His face and neck reddened.

"Unlikely? Why? Don't you think I'm smart enough? Or tough enough? Or is it my religion?" He suddenly flexed the fingers of his right hand.

"You're likely smart enough, and probably tough enough, from what I've heard from your father, but, yes, your religion has much to do with it. The Settlement's Council has never given a PI's license to a Hebrew," I said. "I doubt they are about to change that."

Eli inhaled deeply. "Don't you think I already know that?" He paused and flattened his eyes until they lost all expression. His look became feral. I anticipated the possibility of trouble from him.

"I don't care," he said. "I plan to work in the shadows without a license, just like you."

I hesitated before I answered. I hadn't realized his family, and perhaps his community, too, knew I work unlawfully without the required PI license. I assumed Avram and the others took it for granted I was authorized to be a private investigator. Better, I had hoped they never thought about it at all.

"Working without a license is not an easy way to go, Eli, and it has serious consequences if you're caught." I thought about the constant threat of arrest Chief Inspector Chapman held over my head.

"I know that," he said. His posture remained rigid. I didn't think Eli's potential threat to me had passed.

"Actually," I said, "I don't think you do know it." I paused, looked hard into his eyes, then said, "If you're caught it will mean many years in prison for you. In the meantime, unless you have connections in the Chinese underworld community, you won't get any business from Celestials. You certainly won't get any business from British Shanghailanders or from other western expatriates. Not even me, with my experience, can attract such business.

"That leaves the White Russians in Frenchtown and the Japanese in Hongkew — neither who's likely to give business to a westerner. And, finally, it leaves your own Jewish community, which probably is too small to have enough regular business to sustain you over time."

Eli shook his head slowly. "I know all that, but I still want to work as a private investigator. Will you teach me or are you worried about competition from me?"

My neck grew hot, but I held my tongue and reminded myself that Eli was still young. He had much to learn about decorum and Confucian manners if he was going to succeed in any business in Shanghai. I smiled, slowly shook my head, and, out of respect for his father, offered a solution.

"Here's what I'll do," I said. "Meet me here tomorrow morning at 10:00. Plan to spend most of the day here. I'll give you a few open case files to study while I'm out investigating a new case I've just started.

"When I return, I'll want you to tell me, based on what you've read in the files, what next step you would take to move each case along. Then we'll see."

Eli smiled, as he stood up. "My father said you're *a mentsh — an honorable person*. I'll be here. This is good, Sun-jin. Bless you. This is very good."

"Don't thank me yet. Depending on what you tell me, I might or might not be willing to teach you. Frankly, it will be very time consuming for me if we go forward, so I won't take this on lightly. If you don't have the analytical mind to be a PI, and don't retain most of the facts you will read in the files, I won't have the time to waste on you.

"And one more thing, Eli. Yes, you are correct. I *am working* in the shadows. So don't ever mention this to anyone. And, if I do agree to teach you, you never tell anyone what we're doing. Not anyone. Understood?"

CHAPTER 17

THE CHIEF INSPECTOR SENT FOR me even though I'd barely had time to begin my investigation. Was he looking for a report of my progress so soon?

We met in his office. As I seated myself in front of his desk, he closed the door.

After a few mutually-shared, obligatory Taoist and some British — not very sincere — pleasantries, he nodded at me and said, "Time to call off your investigation, Old Boy. We're closing the file on Sir Victor's kidnapping."

I must have looked confused because I *was* confused. Very confused. Sir Victor was one of the most powerful and influential businessmen in the city. How could I stop searching for him so early into my investigation?

"Has Sir Victor been found?" I asked.

"Found? Not likely. He was never lost, not kidnapped. He's been out of town on a personal matter and never informed anyone, not even his business partners. It was all a misunderstanding.

"We and his partners were wrong in thinking he'd been kidnapped just because we found his comprador's body, and Sir Victor had not been seen or heard from for several weeks. The fact there wasn't a ransom note or other demand should have alerted me."

I frowned. Somehow that explanation didn't seem likely. Then I realized Chapman had never disclosed to me why the SMP had assumed in the first place, when they investigated the comprador's homicide, that Sir Victor had been kidnapped. What reason did they have even to think he'd been with his comprador at *Wing On* when the comprador was killed? Specifically, why did the chief inspector even assume this since there had never been a ransom or other demand-type note from Sir Victor's abductors?

I decided I would pursue this question some other time with the chief inspector. His requirement that I shut down my investigation required my immediate attention.

"Have you now talked to Sir Victor, himself?" I asked. "What did he say about all this?"

"That's not your business, Sun-jin. We won't need you on this case any longer because there is no case. Never was, it seems.

"Get your bill together. I'll arrange to have it paid. I'll also put in a good word for you with Sir Victor when I see him."

"But, sir—"

"No *but*, Sun-jin. It's over. Close your file and move on to one of your other cases." He paused, then smiled. "Discreetly, of course."

CHAPTER 18

I LEFT THE CHIEF INSPECTOR'S OFFICE and walked home. I avoided taking an electric trolley, a rickshaw or a taxi cab. I wanted to use the walk and the time it would take to release the escalating tension I felt, to rid myself of the dark mood that had wrapped itself around me.

I walked slowly, aimlessly, as I pondered the reasons why the chief inspector might have ended my investigation.

I did not believe his explanation. After all, the chief inspector had known there had not been a ransom note or other demand when he hired me, so I did not accept that excuse as his reason. He also knew that Sassoon's disappearance without prior publicity was contrary to the man's typical behavior, so his quiet disappearance should have raised suspicions, not quelled them.

As I walked and looked around me, I realized that my dark mood reflected Shanghai under Japanese occupation. Life in Shanghai — even in the unoccupied treaty concessions — was bleak.

In addition to the ever-increasing overcrowding in the two Round-Eyes' concessions, there now also was the problem of food shortages as more and more Chinese fled the outer districts and poured into the Settlement and Frenchtown to take refuge from the Dwarf Bandits.

It was not that people or merchants were hoarding food. They were not. There wasn't enough food available to hoard because the Kwantung routinely confiscated fruits, vegetables, meat, poultry, and fish from farms where it grew and from junks that brought it to market, as soon as it became available. The Kwantung used this plunder to feed itself.

It was not unusual to see Kwangtung soldiers driving from food stall to food stall in the city, then loading their trucks with most of the groceries and other food found there, leaving very little for the vendor. The Kwantung did not pay for what it took.

My pre-Japanese-occupation method of shopping for groceries each morning, using a basket and rope, no longer worked because of the food shortages.

Gone were the days when I could stand on my fourth-floor balcony and lower a basket to the street out front, have a traveling food vendor fill the basket with the items I'd written on my list, and then haul up the basket, reload it with Yuan to pay for the food, and lower the basket back to the vendor.

I used to repeat that task every morning so that each day's food supply always was fresh. But now the vendors no longer come around because they are not able to stock their traveling carts each morning with enough food to perform the ritual. Even the Black Market has suffered. Its prices have become much too high for people like me to be able to use it.

The only food source regularly available to me (and to most people) these days is at the massive structure known as the

Hongkew Market. This is a three-story-high building that takes up a full city block. It is located across from the Public Gardens, on the other side of the Whangpoo River, near Soochow Creek. There, in normal times, you could buy vegetables, rice, duck tongues, poultry, fish, chicken feet and beaks, meat, and fruit, all in abundance, at all hours of the day and night. Now, under the Occupation, its stock of food is limited so that I've rarely been able to obtain most of what I want in one trip when I go there. Now, I have to visit the market three or even four times each week in hopes of having enough to eat for me, Mei-hua, and Bik.

After remaining at home for a few hours, and drinking some beer to assuage my black mood, I left my flat, bringing Bik with me on her leash. We boarded a rickshaw. I would ride it to the Public Gardens and walk across the Garden Bridge to the Hongkew Market to buy food.

I wasn't thrilled about walking across the Garden Bridge because recently the Dwarf Bandits had started encouraging Hongkew's residents to arm themselves with clubs and to beat any Chinese they came upon in the streets of the district. Fortunately, the market is only a few hundred meters from the bridge, so I hoped we would be able to make it there and back without incident. Fortunately, I hadn't yet had a problem during my many visits there.

I had another concern about walking across the Garden Bridge to Hongkew. I'd heard rumors that the Kwangtung has recently been stopping and harassing Celestials as we try to cross from one side of the Whangpoo River to the other. This had not been the situation during my other visits to the market.

If the rumors were true, however, I hoped the presence of Bik with me would cause the Dwarf Bandits to view me with some friendliness, if not compassion.

Bik and I stepped from the rickshaw and crossed the Public Gardens without incident. I'd been careful the whole time to watch out for SMP constables who, adhering to the Settlement's strict race laws set out in the Land Regulations, might stop me to check my papers and to remind me that neither dogs nor Chinese (other than *Amahs* with their Round-Eyes charges) are allowed in the Public Gardens.

As Bik and I approached the bridge, I saw a long line at the Settlement side of the entrance. Apparently, the rumors were true. The Dwarf Bandits were treating Shanghai as if it were their own city. They were stopping people as they crossed the bridge to check their papers and to otherwise inconvenience them.

As we slowly eased our way forward in line, Bik and I were very hot. The sun beat down on us since there were no trees or other obstacles to cast cooling shade on the bridge. I was sorry I'd brought Bik with me. She was suffering from the heat, and panted continuously. Her long pink tongue lolled from the corner of her mouth.

I had worn a coolie-type straw hat with a wide brim that shaded my head and face, keeping me relatively cool. Every few minutes I removed my hat and fanned Bik to cool her. I swear she smiled at me each time I did that.

As we edged our way forward in line, every once in a while a Dwarf-Bandit soldier, puffed-up with vanity, would strut along the waiting line, loudly reading a proclamation to us.

His Chinese-language skills were dreadful so I had difficulty understanding him. But because he repeated his performance so often I finally pieced together enough of what he said to understand that the proclamation ordered all people in line to show respect to the soldiers by engaging in a gentle bow and a polite statement of *Good morning,* or some similar greeting, when a soldier was nearby.

As the soldier with the proclamation turned around from the far end of the line and moved back alongside me, I bowed slightly and stated the mandated greeting.

An old man ahead of me in the line, however, refused to do so, even when the soldier stopped and ordered him to bow. The soldier, acting like a mad dog, shouted in Japanese at the old man, their faces only inches apart.

When the old man continued to refuse to obey — if he even understood what the soldier was screaming at him — the Dwarf Bandit slapped him hard across his face, causing the old man's wire-rim eyeglasses to fly off his face and to shatter nearby. The blow knocked the old man to the ground.

Two other soldiers immediately ran up, shouted something in Japanese I couldn't understand, grabbed the old man by his arms, and dragged him from the bridge, back to the Public Gardens.

As Bik and I slowly moved across the bridge, I thought about how much Hongkew has changed since the beginning of our undeclared war with Japan. According to a report recently printed in the *Shanghai Times*, many of Hongkew's original Dwarf-Bandit residents have left the district and have returned to Japan. It seems the fighting in Hongkew had destroyed their homes and businesses, leveling many city blocks from repeated bombings.

As a result of this evacuation by its original Dwarf-Bandit residents, and the desire of the Kwantung to repopulate Little Tokyo (as this part of Hongkew is popularly known), a new type Dwarf Bandit has taken the place of those former inhabitants. These new people are gangsters, soldiers, and adventurers who are out to exploit the Dwarf-Bandit's victory in the Battle of Shanghai. In contrast to the district's former Dwarf-Bandit shopkeepers and tradesmen, these people are an unsettled population, indifferent to the city, to this district in particular, and to Hongkew's small, native Celestial population, as well as to the Hebrews in Little Vienna.

Bik and I stood in line for more than one hour before we came to a table set up in the middle of the bridge.

I handed over my papers, bowed slightly, and said, *Good morning.*

One of the sentries looked at Bik, then said in badly spoken Shanghainese *Hu*, "Nice dog. We eat dog when we find them. Best meal for hungry soldier. Better keep an eye on that handsome dog." He looked me in my eyes and licked his lips.

I said nothing. I tightened my grip on Bik's leash, retrieved my papers from the soldier behind the table, and quickly walked to the Hongkew Market, without another incident.

After we returned home, I put a bowl of water and some food outside for Bik, and turned her loose. As I turned to go back up the stairs to my flat, I noticed two large men swiftly approaching me. Not just approaching in my general direction, but approaching me specifically. Their eyes were fixed on mine as they came closer.

My back stiffened. I reflexively and mentally assumed a *Shaolin* defensive fighting posture, pouring the weight from my left leg into my right leg, as I subtlety moved it back behind my now-empty left leg.

When the two men were almost on top of me, they abruptly stopped walking.

"Mr. Ling?" one said. "Are you Ling Sun-jin?"

"*Ayeeyah!* Who wants to know?" I shifted my eyes from one of the men to the other, then back again.

"Sir Victor Sassoon would like to talk with you. If it is convenient, he would prefer we bring you to him immediately." The man slightly bowed his head.

I raised my eyebrows, then frowned.

One of the men said, "Sir Victor is at his office at Sassoon House. We can ride together in our automobile." He pointed toward a dark green 1931 Cord touring car parked at the curb, not far from my flat.

CHAPTER 19

Eli Ben-David Reuben had quietly joined the CCP in 1937, shortly after his twenty-third birthday, when he witnessed, on several occasions, the inefficiency and corruption of Chiang Kai-shek's KMT political party, and the cruelty and corruption of Chiang's Nationalist KMT army.

Eli knew firsthand the ruthlessness of Chiang's private army, known to everyone as the Blue Shirts, a group Chiang had deliberately (so he proudly boasted to newspapers) modeled after the Nazi thugs known as the Brown Shirts. Eli hadn't been in Shanghai for more than seven months when the Blue Shirts caught him out in the street one night, beat him, and called him, "Filthy Jew," among other similar epithets.

One month later, Eli joined the CCP to take part in the fight against Chiang and his KMT.

Eli was a quiet, studious CCP revolutionary. He did not march with other members; he did not make or throw bombs; he carried no weapon other than a sharp pencil, a notepad, and his incisive mind and memory. His role in preparing for the coming revolution, a role he carved out for himself, was to write, edit, and publish the CCP's underground local weekly newspaper, *Slovo — The Word.*

In the meantime, however, he recognized that he had to earn a living. So, he decided, he would become a private investigator like his father's friend, Ling Sun-jin, working without a license and without a gun permit among members of Shanghai's underworld and Jewish communities.

Eli looked at his gold Elgin wrist watch, a present from his parents when they still lived happily in Breslau.

12:40 pm. She was late.

Eli stood in the shadows of rare huanghuali trees, not far from Shanghai's Baby Drawer, and kept his eyes and ears alert to the possible coming of Japanese soldiers, who regularly patrolled this area.

He heard a noise to his left.

He crouched slightly as he peered into the distant brush. Then he saw her.

He straightened up to his full height so she could see him.

"I'm here," he whispered. He smiled and waved his arm to attract her attention.

She rushed over to him, kissed him on the cheek, and hugged him.

"Good to see you," Mei-hua said. "I've missed you." She took his hand in hers as they walk away together.

CHAPTER 20

"HAI, GENERAL," JMP INSPECTOR DETECTIVE Harue said. He clicked his heals together and saluted the officer seated behind the desk he faced.

"Ah! Inspector Detective Harue. Sit, please." The general pointed at a chair facing his desk, and nodded. "I have an assignment for you."

Harue maintained the severe, stoic facial expression he always displayed when in the presence of authority. Inside, however, his heart raced. *At last*, he thought. *I'm being given my chance to prove my worth.*

"Your men are doing well keeping order and policing the Emperor's enemies. Your success has been noted in your file. I want you to continue to engage in that task even though I am going to add a new aspect to that assignment."

"Yes, sir." Harue worked to slow down his breathing. He did not want to seem too anxious to take on an additional assignment, although he was so hungry for one and had lobbied so long to achieve it. He could taste the glory it surely would bring him.

"It is time to put pressure on the Round-Eyes in the Settlement and French Concession, to remind them of our nation's power, that we can march in and take control of their treaty concessions any time we wish to do so." The general stared hard at Harue.

Harue nodded, but said nothing. His previous experience with this man informed him that the general liked to be listened to, not spoken to, not even in response to some point he'd just made.

"I want you to commence the continuing practice of arresting and holding in custody those Chinese refugees, from other parts of the city, who have taken refuge behind the walls the Round-Eyes have constructed around their concessions. My purpose is to convince the refugees to not leave the concessions for any reason, not even to work.

"If they do leave the concessions, however, you will arrest them and, specifically, will intimidate them. I want these people to be afraid to come out from behind the walls once they've arrived there."

"*Hai*," Harue said.

"You should take our recent experience in Nanking as your model. I want these people to fear the Kwantung. You should intimidate them so they will remain inside the concessions, fearful of leaving for even a short period for fear of being arrested by you.

"My goal is to crowd the concessions, and to strain the Round-Eyes' resources so as to make life in the concessions as unbearable as possible for the Round-Eyes, who will have to care for the Chinese vermin within their territories."

Harue smiled.

"At the same time, unless absolutely necessary for some other reason, I want you to avoid arresting any Chinese who attempts to enter one of the concessions. Indeed, you should encourage the Chinese you meet to flee to the concessions to avoid your cruelty. Warn them of the dangers of leaving the concessions once they have entered there."

Harue saluted. He would be pleased to squeeze the Round-Eyes by packing their concessions full of filthy, uneducated Chinese, until the treaty concessions could hold no more. Then he would drive more in.

"Of course, Inspector Detective, I also expect you to be vigilant in discovering spies for the KMT or CCP who might harm our cause."

Harue saluted, nodded, stood up, and bowed deeply.

CHAPTER 21

I LOOKED AT THE TWO MEN Sassoon had sent to fetch me. I considered my options.

I preferred to avoid Sassoon if possible. My previous encounters with him had all been harmful to me. I disliked him for having destroyed my career with the SMP. At least that was how I saw it. Chief Inspector Chapman would probably disagree with that assessment. He likely would say I destroyed my own career with the SMP by not following his direct order concerning Sassoon. We would both be right.

I also considered Sassoon — like all wealthy Round-Eyes — to be a criminal, if only indirectly. Or, if not an actual criminal himself, I thought of him as someone who was on the fringe of crime, as someone who used his power, wealth, and other people to perform his questionable deeds, whatever they might be. I couldn't think of any at the moment.

But, I thought, *why should I let that bother me? I deal every day with criminal triad-members. They are a large part of my private- investigator clientele.* Reality had set in for me.

The decision to go with these two men wasn't hard to make. You do not defy and insult a man with Sassoon's power. When someone like Sir Victor summons you to him, no matter how polite his invitation might be, you do not refuse. It isn't really an invitation. It's a summons, a command.

"Let's go," I said, resigned to my circumstances. I turned and walked toward the touring car.

Sir Victor looked at me and smiled.

"It seems, Mr. Ling, we cannot avoid one another," he said, as I accepted his invitation to sit across the desk from him. "What's it been now? Four or five years? Perhaps six, even?

"Call me Sun-jin," I said.

We were sitting in his office on the top floor of Sassoon House, that combination shopping emporium and office building located at 20 Nanking Road, not far from the Bund, and not far from *Wing On* department store.

It had been many years since I'd visited Sassoon here. That visit had been my undoing at the SMP.

Sir Victor reached across his desk and opened his humidor. He pulled out a cigar for himself and turned the open box toward me. He nodded, indicating I could take one.

"No thanks," I said, shaking my head. "Excellent-quality cigars are wasted on me." I recalled the last visit to this office when Sassoon had bragged to me that his cigars had been specially made for him in Cuba.

This also was quite a change from that last time I was here when Sir Victor had taken a cigar for himself, had made a big point of cutting its tip and then lighting it, but had not offered me one. I had not been a welcomed visitor to his office that day.

I decided I would take the first step toward reconciliation.

"I was glad to learn from Chief Inspector Chapman that

you had not been kidnapped, that it was all an innocent misunderstanding."

One of his eyebrows lifted. "That's a nice sentiment, Mr. Ling, but it isn't true. I was kidnapped."

"But the chief inspector told me it was a misunderstanding, that you—"

Sir Victor held up his palm to quiet me. "The chief inspector was mistaken. I was kidnapped and was held for a little more than five weeks."

I continued, my confusion evident to anyone paying attention. "But he told me you were away from Shanghai on business. Wasn't that true?"

"That wasn't true. I was forcibly held in Chapei. At least I suspect it was Chapei."

I decided to change the subject before he started to think I was questioning his honesty.

"Why did you send for me, Sir Victor? How can I help you?"

I waited while he drew heavily on his cigar, held the smoke in his mouth for a few seconds, then streamed it out toward the ceiling. It seemed to me he was organizing his thoughts.

He did not answer my question.

"Here's the strange part, Mr. Ling. The kidnappers did not want a ransom from me. In fact, it seems they didn't want anything at all from me. At least nothing that I could give them.

"I was pretty much in the position to give them anything they might have wanted, but it seemed they didn't care.

"I offered them $5 million to let me go, but they weren't interested. Then I offered $10 million. Still no interest. Then, after about five weeks, without any explanation or any demand made of me, they set me free late one night."

"That's very odd," I said. "So, Sir Victor, may I ask you again, why did you send for me? How can I help you?"

"I want to hire you. I'll pay you well, and I'll be greatly indebted to you. I want you to investigate the kidnapping, find out who did it, and, most important, find out why they did it since it obviously wasn't for money or something else I could give them."

This intrigued me, but I wasn't interested. All my experiences so far with Sir Victor had turned out bad for me. I didn't need another poor experience with him. Somehow, I had to extricate myself from his request and offer without offending him.

I shook my head. "Sorry, Sir Victor, but I have a full load of work right now. I cannot just drop those cases to take yours, now that I know you're not in any danger. You'll have to find someone else. I'm sure the chief inspector will be able to recommend—"

"Perhaps you didn't understand, Mr. Ling. I'm not asking you to investigate this. I'm telling you to do so." He frowned.

"No, sir, I do understand. Perfectly. And I'm telling you that—"

Sassoon slammed his fist on the desk. His face darkened. He spoke quietly, menacingly, much more softly than a few seconds ago. The threat was in his soft tone.

"You will do this for me, Ling, or I will ruin you. You will never work in Shanghai again, not legally, not illegally." He paused, looked into my eyes, and held my stare. "You'll be finished here."

He relit his cigar, and said, "We're done here. You need to get to work solving my kidnapping."

I remained seated and stared at him.

He eventually looked up again. "Well? Now what?"

"I'll need your help with two aspects of this."

"Go on."

"You must intervene with Chief Inspector Chapman so he knows I'm working on this case at your request. He must not block me or punish me because I'm pursuing this in the open, without a private investigator's license and without a gun permit. This is necessary because there won't be any way I can work on this for you without it being known by the SMP and others.

"I'll also need Chapman's cooperation with my investigation. I'll want all evidence the SMP found when they briefly investigated your kidnapping, and the homicide files from your comprador's case. No withholding of information by the cops."

"Consider it done," Sassoon said.

"And there's one other thing," I added.

Sassoon frowned. "You said two things, not three. Now what?"

"When this is completed, whether or not I'm successful, I want your word you will use your influence to have my PI's license and my weapon's permit reinstated. You know, the ones you blocked before, after you had me fired from the SMP."

"That's not going to happen," Sassoon said.

PART TWO

CHAPTER 22

THE NEXT MORNING, SOMEONE IN Sassoon's office called to say that Sir Victor had spoken with the chief inspector, who agreed to cooperate with me in all respects.

"Does that mean I can carry a weapon?" I said.

"Sir Victor said that Chapman will cooperate with you in all respects. You decide what that means."

I rang off the telephone to think about how I would proceed with the investigation.

I still was annoyed that Sir Victor and, by extension, the chief inspector had forced me to take on Sassoon's case without regard to whether or not I cared to do so. It seemed that, as before with the chief inspector and the murder of the nightclub singer called the Yellow Swan, I was being used as his and, by extension, as Sassoon's plaything to be manipulated as they saw fit.

I took a deep breath, then another, and took stock of my anger. I noted it for future reference, and set it aside. I decided that since I had no choice but to proceed, I would do my best to accommodate Sir Victor in all respects. Hopefully, when this was done, I will have earned Sir Victor's gratitude. Doing so would make my life in Shanghai much better than it has been since I was fired from the SMP.

I telephoned the chief inspector. I thanked him for offering to cooperate with me, then asked him to tell me everything he knew about the kidnapping.

"I can come to the central station to meet with you if you do not want to discuss this over the telephone," I said.

"That won't be necessary," he replied. "I don't know anything about the kidnapping other than this: I did not learn about the kidnapping in connection with our investigation of the murder. That came later. I learned of it when Sir Victor's business partners approached me to say they had not heard from him for about five weeks. At first, even after learning that, we never considered the possibility that he'd been abducted. We assumed that Sir Victor had had some reason to disappear, a reason we did not know about."

"Why would Sir Victor's business partners be worried enough to call his absence to the attention of the SMP?" I asked. "After all, Sir Victor is a world-renowned businessman and traveler. I suspect he often leaves Shanghai for trips — especially business trips — and does not tell people that he's going."

"Actually, you're wrong about that. According to his partners, Sir Victor always informs them where they can reach him in the event of some crisis in the market or in his business or affecting their investments together. He didn't do that this time."

I briefly considered this. "What, then, made them think he was kidnapped, that he hadn't just changed his way of dealing with them," I said, "or have some private mission he didn't want them to know about?"

"I don't know. That's something you will have to follow up with them or with Sir Victor."

I thought about that, then said, "So, Chief Inspector, tell me, why did *you* think Sir Victor had been kidnapped and had not just voluntarily disappeared?"

"Because when he reappeared in Shanghai, Sir Victor said he'd been kidnapped. That's good enough for me."

"But you thought that before Sir Victor reappeared. That's why you hired me to find him."

"I have to go now," he said. "I have a police department to run."

We ended the call. Unfortunately, the chief inspector's limited information did not give me much to get started with. It appeared, for now at least, I was completely on my own.

I normally begin the investigation of a crime by looking at the police records. I examine the autopsy and laboratory reports in the case of a homicide. I look at photographs of the crime scene. I pour over the reports of initial interviews of witnesses conducted by the first constables on the scene. I study the other reports prepared by the inspector detectives who later show up to investigate and who conduct their own interviews.

"That wasn't possible in the instance of Sassoon's kidnapping since the police — other than the chief inspector and a few other high-level Special Branch officers he'd disclosed the crime to — were not made aware of the kidnapping.

There was a police file relating to the comprador's murder investigation. Chapman told me there was no police file concerning Sir Victor's kidnapping, at least there was none that was disclosed to me by him. I was aware, however, that the SMP sometimes creates secret files involving sensitive cases. There might be such a file in Sassoon's case.

I arranged to borrow the murder file. I hoped I might see something there — something missed by the SMP inspector detectives who had no idea they also should have been looking at the same evidence with regard to a kidnapping. I looked forward to receiving that file.

There is something else I typically do in an investigation that I could not do in this one because there was no kidnapping file. I usually try to construct a timeline. This enables me to see and think about the investigation as a whole, beginning sometime before the occurrence of the crime, and moving through to the date I am considering that information.

Since this investigatory device usually resulted from information found in the police reports, I was unable to do that in this inquiry. One of my goals, therefore, would be for me to develop a timeline from evidence I uncovered, however scanty that data might be.

I should go back and interview Sassoon now, I thought. *Maybe he'll be able to shed some light on the sequence of events if I frame my questions in that context.*

I thought more about this. Actually, I doubted Sassoon would be very helpful, that I would learn much new from him I hadn't learned from the chief inspector, but I would have to give it a try. My options right now were limited. I couldn't afford to ignore any possible avenue of investigation, including any possible discrepancies between what the chief inspector told me and what I might now learn from Sir Victor, even as they might recite the same facts. It was possible their emphasis would differ. That, in itself, might be useful.

I thought, *Even if I succeed in constructing a time sequence based on what Sassoon might tell me, that sequence would not amount to much on its own.*

But it would be a start. And this is how you build investigations. Piece by piece, all leading to a whole — positive and negative, Yin and Yang — that allow you to complete and solve the puzzle through facts, intuition, experience, gossip, and, especially, good *joss*.

The most important thing I could not do in this investigation, unfortunately, my greatest obstacle in this quest, was to observe the crime scene of the murder and the kidnapping — the scene outside *Wing On* department store. Too much time had gone by since these crimes occurred to make anything I might now see at the sidewalk meaningful.

But I wasn't discouraged by that. I knew there might not have been a lot to observe at the original crime scene even had I been able to look around soon after the two crimes took place.

Yet visiting an undisturbed crime setting has other, often intangible, benefits for the investigator, including one intangible that non-PIs and non-cops have trouble understanding because they've never experienced it.

When you're at a crime scene, you spend time absorbing the feel of the crime and the sense of the site where the crime occurred. You try to imagine it occurring or even to see it as the victim saw it as it occurred or, perhaps, as the criminal might have seen it when the crime occurred. This is so whether you are a SMP Special Branch inspector detective, as I had been, or you are a PI, as I now am. This feeling you get grows out of experience and the intuition you develop as an investigator, intuition that experience brings about and nourishes.

So, as part of my investigation, sometime soon, I planned to visit the sidewalk outside the *Wing On* entrance to try to absorb whatever remaining message the crime scene might offer me, if any.

Since I was under pressure to solve this investigation quickly, I wondered if I should involve Eli as my assistant. He certainly had performed well with the files I'd given him as a learning example, demonstrating to me when I questioned him that he'd been thorough when he read them, that his memory was excellent, that his instincts were good, and that his reasoning was powerful. All he lacked was experience. I could find ways to give him that through exposure to me.

CHAPTER 23

BIG-EARED TU RECEIVED DAILY REPORTS from Hong Kong indicating his wives were safe and were thriving under the indirect protection of the British, who ran that city, as well as under the watchful eyes of the Green Gang members he'd sent to Hong Kong to act as his wives' body guards.

After one week hiding in Shanghai from the Kwantung, Tu became reasonably satisfied he could leave the shadows and safely return to the open. The immediate threat against him had subsided because the Dwarf Bandits in that short time had so much strengthened their garrison that they no longer saw Tu's network of spies as a threat to their occupation of the city. This viewpoint was nourished by Tu's Green Gang members who distributed a significant amount of *squeeze* among senior Kwantung officers to ensure Tu's safety.

Tu moved back to Frenchtown. He and his second, third, and fourth wives relocated into a replacement house located at 888 Rue du Consulat, not far from Shanghai's largest Chinese-owned gambling club — the *Collective Prosperity Club* — where, every day, hordes of Celestial men and women wasted hours for the opportunity to leave behind their hard-earned wages.

Tu insisted that his new home be located at 888 Rue du Consulat, the site of an existing dwelling, so he could have the advantage — three times over — of the number "8" which everyone knows is a lucky number. To achieve this, Tu arranged with the reluctant, but pliable, former owner of the building at this address to buy the house and land from him. Tu then had the house updated with several guard towers and a perimeter barbed-wire fence installed.

As a sign of respect and obedience, when Tu acquired his new residence, gifts in the form of rugs, calligraphy scrolls, paintings, curios, and furniture poured in from, among others, Chiang Kai-shek, Chiang's brother-in-law and finance minister, T. V. Soong, Pock-Marked Huang, General Dai Li, from many high-placed leaders of several triads, from Chief Inspector Chapman, from Lord Cornell Franklin, and from several Shanghai businessmen — including Victor Sassoon.

Tu armed his brick mansion as if it were a fortress. Members of the Green Gang guarded the house and grounds day and night, as if their lives depended on their diligence and success.

Tu was determined to use his espionage network to root-out secret members of the CCP who, he believed, were working to undermine Chiang and the KMT for their own advantage after the war with Japan ended. He also was determined to sabotage the Kwantung's war efforts in occupied Shanghai, but that goal was secondary to harming the CCP and protecting the Republic.

Tu assigned Frenchtown's police chief, Pock-Marked Huang, to run his network of spies for him.

Huang sat in Tu's Great Room smoking a *Double Dragon*-brand cigarette.

"I have identified several previously unknown CCP members living in our city," Huang said. "We will continue to watch them to see if they are engaged in spying or in other operations that counter the KMT's objectives or otherwise undermine the odious truce that Chiang and that weasel, Mao, entered into at Xi'an."

Tu nodded, then looked across the room at his caged songbirds. He enjoyed their songs. He certainly enjoyed taking them for walks at sunrise every day and setting them free to fly, while he gossiped with other songbird owners.

He turned back to face Huang.

"Of these eight Communists bandits you named in this paper," Tu said, as he extended his hand with the list toward Huang, "I noticed one is a woman."

"Yes, only one, but she is a very interesting one. I was going to discuss her with you separately because I think you will find her intriguing."

Huang drew heavily on his cigarette, held its smoke in his lungs while he composed his thoughts, then turned his head away from Tu, and exhaled the smoke. He turned back to face Tu.

"Her name is Wu Mei-hua. She is the daughter of a KMT colonel. She now works for the KMT in the Ministry of Justice."

Tu rang a small bell that had been sitting on the table between him and Huang. A servant entered with *chota hazra — a pot of tea and two pieces of toast with jam*. He placed sipping bowls in front of Tu and Huang.

After the servant poured the tea and left, Huang said, "This Mei-hua used to be an ardent Communist. She even accompanied Mao for part of the way on the Long March. When she returned home to recover from the illness that caused her to leave Mao's bandits, she publicly renounced the CCP in a letter she sent to the *North-China Daily News.*

"She claimed she'd given up all her ties to the CCP, that she'd seen the foolishness of her previous life, and that she had taken a job with the KMT to be an obedient daughter and to aid Chiang in his fight to save China from the Dwarf Bandits and the CCP.

"No one believed her recantation. Everyone knew her father had pressured her into renouncing the Communist vermin to further his own career in the army, and that he's obtained the job for her to encourage the illusion she wished to sustain."

Tu nodded and slid his hands up the long sleeves of his Mandarin gown.

"The renunciation and KMT job are perfect covers for spying," Tu said. "I recall reading her letter to the newspaper. At the time, I believed her words sounded false. I didn't take her retraction seriously. Continue to watch her. I don't trust her. We might have to eliminate her at some point."

CHAPTER 24

MEI-HUA AND I, ALONG WITH Bik, who was hooked onto her leash, rode a taxi from my flat to the Willow Pattern Tea House to share a pot of tea and then to eat dinner. Bik would have her own meal there. We'd brought her food along with us.

The Willow Pattern Tea House was constructed during the Ming Dynasty. It sits on pilings in the middle of the Whangpoo River. The tea house can be reached only by walking across the Bridge of Nine Turnings, a meandering wooden bridge having abrupt right and left turns designed to keep out evil spirits who, as everyone knows, always prefer to travel in a straight line.

We settled into a private room and sat on pillows on the floor facing each another. We were separated by a low, legless table on which sat a tea caddy filled with dried yellow tea leaves. Next to it were a tea scoop, an urn of boiled, pure spring water, two bowls without handles which we would hold with both hands as we sipped our tea, and a lighted candle.

"*Ayeeyah!* I want to bring you up to date on my new investigation," I said. "I can't go into detail because I've agreed to keep it confidential, but it involves a crime committed against Sir Victor Sassoon."

I paused to think how I wanted to say this to Mei-hua, and to gauge her reaction to what I'd said so far. She gave nothing away. Her face remained inscrutable. I had no idea how she might feel about me working for Sassoon after how he'd treated me six years ago.

"It's one of those situations where Sir Victor has ordered me to investigate this for him, telling me that things will not go well for me if I refuse."

Mei-hua did not hold back her feelings.

"Oh, Sun-jin. Be careful. You know how dangerous he can be. He might turn on you at any time. I don't trust him. You shouldn't either."

I held up my palm to quiet her. I nodded.

"I understand. But it might even be worse than that. I suspect things will not go well for me even if I carry on the investigation, but am not successful, although Sir Victor never said that."

Mei-hua reached across the table and took my hand. "Why are you telling me this?"

"I'm worried my involvement in this could place you in danger."

"Me? How could—"

I held up my palm again. "*Qing — Please*, Mei-hua. All in good time. Allow me to finish."

She nodded, but released my hand.

"The crime I'm investigating is a serious one. It unfolded in a most unusual way. And even though I do not yet understand why it occurred or why it evolved as it did, the very nature of the act committed against Sir Victor tells me he has very powerful enemies.

"It is not impossible for me to imagine that such enemies

might threaten to harm you in order to influence me to drop the investigation or to intentionally perform it poorly."

Mei-hua turned up her eyeballs and showed me the whites of her eyes. This is a traditional response we Chinese call *Giving Someone White Eyes*. We do this to show our distain for the other person.

"That seems far-fetched," Mei-hua said. She picked up her tea bowl and slurped the tea, all the while staring into my eyes over the lip of the bowl.

"I would like you to leave Shanghai," I said, "and temporarily live somewhere else, perhaps in Hong Kong, until my investigation is over."

"No. I will not—"

"Mei-hua, listen to me. This is probably a good time for you to do so, in any event, with all the chaos being created here by the Dwarf Bandits. In Hong Kong, you will be among British Round-Eyes, so you will be safe."

"No, Sun-jin. Shanghai is my home. I will not leave. I will deal with Sir Victor's enemies should it come to that. Besides, I am more likely to be in danger from my father's enemies in the CCP, because he is a KMT officer, and from my own enemies in the CCP, because I renounced my membership in the Party, than I am likely to be from Victor Sassoon's enemies."

"*Qivng rang — Excuse me*, Mei-hua," I said. "Accommodate me this one time. Anything could happen to you during this state of war we find ourselves in. If something happens to you it would be easy to blame it on the war, and no one would be any the wiser for it."

She shook her head. "My mind is made up, Sun-jin. I will not flee Shanghai."

CHAPTER 25

MEI-HUA AND I SPENT A tense night at her flat after we left the tea house. The subject of her leaving Shanghai did not come up again. In the morning, I left Bik with her, then headed home. I bathed and changed my clothes, pomaded my hair, then headed to my office.

I decided I needed to interview Sassoon, after all, just as I would interview any witness or question any other victim of a crime. I would do this even though he'd indicated, when I called to set up the meeting, that he thought this would be a waste of time because he didn't know anything now he hadn't already told me.

"What do you mean you want to meet?" Sassoon had said when I called him. "We met yesterday. Wasn't that enough?"

I ended the call without answering his question. I was running this investigation, not him. I would have to make that clear when we met.

We got together in his office twenty minutes later. He was not pleased to see me.

"Why are we meeting again? You're wasting time," he said,

as soon as I sat down. "Wasting my time and yours. You should be out investigating the kidnapping."

There are interview techniques I learned when I was an inspector detective that are used when you are faced with a stubbornly resistant witness or a stubbornly resistant crime victim. Sir Victor qualified on all three grounds. He was a victim, a witness, and he certainly was stubbornly resistant.

I would take my time with him, apply one of the most successful techniques I've used in similar past situations, and, hopefully, find out something useful from him. Successful investigations, I learned long ago, are constructed with patience and with little steps. They rarely, if ever, are made from lightning strikes.

"Sir Victor, please, indulge me. This is how I have conducted hundreds of successful investigations."

He nodded and frowned, but remained silent.

"I want you to take me through all the events from the time you and your comprador entered *Wing On*, until you later were released by the kidnappers. Tell me everything, even if it doesn't seem important."

"I told all that to the chief inspector. Didn't he tell you? What's the matter with you people?"

"He did tell me. His version, at least. His second-hand version. I need to hear it directly from you, from your perspective," I said, "to see if I interpret your information the same way the chief inspector did."

I shrugged, stopped talking, and stared hard at one of the most ruthless and powerful men in Shanghai.

He stared back.

I folded my hands on my lap and waited. I thought of the

saying, *wei wu wei*, the Taoist view that one must always permit things to take their own course, not force them.

"You're wasting time," Sassoon finally said.

I shrugged again and remained silent. I continued staring at him.

Wei wu wei.

While this battle of wills continued, I thought about what little I had learned about the case from the chief inspector. Then I took this limited information, while I waited for Sassoon to speak, and mentally placed it into one of four logic baskets: things about the case I know; things I don't know; things I don't know, but I can reasonably assume based on other information and logic; and, things I want to know. Altogether, they were not very much.

Sassoon suddenly spoke and broke into my thoughts. His soft voice masked intense anger that was apparent to me from the sudden, ruddy color of his neck and face. He clenched his hands into tight fists as he spoke.

"My comprador and I went to a meeting with the president of *Wing On*. We met in his office on the top floor of the department store. I wanted to buy the real property so I could tear down the building and build a luxury hotel on the site. He wasn't interested, wouldn't even consider the possibility of moving his business to another location, so we left.

"As we stepped from the building and walked across the sidewalk, someone behind me suddenly threw a cloth hood over my head, drew it closed under my chin, and, in doing so, blinded me."

"Who knew you and your comprador would be at *Wing On?*" I said.

"The two of us, and my secretary who set up the meeting

with *Wing On*'s president. Obviously, the president knew, too. I don't know if he told anyone."

I made a mental note to meet with *Wing On*'s president. "Go on," I said.

"As I struggled to rip off the hood, I heard my comprador shouting, *Taipan, Taipan*. He sounded as if he was warning me about something.

"Then I was pushed from my back and pulled from my front into an automobile. I heard the door slam. We drove off."

"How many men were there?"

Sassoon slowly shook his head. "I never saw them, and don't know. As I said, one of them put a hood over my head. It had to be more than one person though, probably at least three, because the two shots I heard occurred while I was being pushed by one person and dragged by another to the car. At least three people, I would say, possibly four, if someone else was the driver."

"Did they say anything?"

"No."

"Did they have accents?"

"I don't know."

"Were they Round-Eyes? Celestials? Dwarf Bandits?"

He shook his head again. "They never spoke to me or spoke in my presence. Not from the time they first put the hood over my head until they set me free in Chapei."

"Do you know where they took you, where the room was?"

"No, but they later turned me loose in Chapei, so maybe the room was there."

"Tell me about the room?"

"It was always dark. I know it was above ground because we walked up five steps to get to it after we entered a building.

"What happened after you arrived at the room?"

"I was chained to a bed. They removed the hood from my head, but the only person in the room with me at any time wore his own head covering. I lost track of time because the shades were drawn on the only window. As I said, the room was always dark."

"Did you ever hear their voices once you arrived there or ever see their faces?"

"No. I already told you that. Neither. They never spoke to me. They wrote messages to me on a small blackboard they carried into the room with them when they entered.

"Whenever they came into the room, whichever person came in, wore a balaclava, then put my hood over my head so I couldn't see their face. But I know there were three of them from the different times they entered the room. I could sense the differences in their sizes from the sound of their footsteps."

"Did they harm you in any way?" I said.

"No. They were always polite. They never even threatened me. As I told you, I offered them a ransom to let me loose, but they wrote on the chalk board that they had no interest in my money. Not even when I increased the amount of the offer."

"Did they indicate they wanted something besides money?"

"No."

This had me stumped. It's pretty hard to solve a mystery if you do not know the motive of the criminal. So far, this seemed to be a crime without any purpose.

"What else?" I asked.

"Nothing."

"You're sure?" I said.

He hesitated, but nodded. "One day, without any explanation, they put the hood over my head again, but this time they walked me down the five steps and outside to a car. They set me loose in Chapei. It was late at night. They never told me the reason for that or, for that matter, for any of it.

"Can you think of anything else, no matter how trivial it might seem?" I said.

"No. I've told you everything I remember." He slowly shook his head and frowned as if I were a recalcitrant child. "Now, get back to work."

I left Sassoon's office and went to the lobby of Sassoon House. There I used a telephone to call the president of *Wing On*. I made an appointment to see him.

CHAPTER 26

I SPENT THE NIGHT WITH MEI-HUA at her flat. Neither of us mentioned Hong Kong again. I did not tell her about my meeting with Sassoon.

When I left in the morning to go home, I took Bik with me. It was the beginning of my week to be with her. That meant Mei-hua would spend most nights this week at my flat.

At home, I shaved, showered, groomed my hair, changed my clothes, and hooked Bik up to her collar and leash. We walked to the electric trolley stop, hopped aboard the first one to come along without Kwantung troops aboard, then rode the streetcar to a stop several blocks from my office. We would both enjoy the short walk to Bubbling Well Road before we settled down inside.

When Bik and I left the streetcar we walked along the Bund, passing by such imperious granite buildings as the Shanghai Club, the Hongkong & Shanghai Bank, the Customs House, and other imposing edifices, none of which I've ever entered, and likely never will enter.

We stopped at the corner of Foochow Road to wait for the signal from the Sikh, who stood on a box in the intersection, directing traffic. As soon as he blew his whistle and waved his traffic flag to signal us to cross, Bik pulled on her leash and led me through the intersection toward the other side.

As I passed the Sikh, we nodded to each other and smiled. We've engaged in this ritual for more than one year now, ever since he was assigned to this intersection.

Bik and I were almost to the curb when she yanked the leash and pulled me out of the way of a speeding automobile. It did not slow down after almost running us over. The Sikh sprinted to us.

"Are you all right, sir?" he said. He put his hand on my shoulder to steady me.

I shook my head, no. "I didn't see that," I said. "My dog saved me." I knelt and patted Bik's head.

"That automobile never slowed down," the policeman said. "In fact, sir, I would swear it sped up and swerved toward you as you neared the curb."

He turned and looked in the direction the car had fled. "I do believe that the automobile attempted to run you down."

CHAPTER 27

THE OVERALL POLITICAL, ECONOMIC, AND humanitarian situation in Shanghai continued to deteriorate under the Dwarf Bandits' occupation. Coolies and peasants from outside the city and from the Chinese districts within the city fled to the International Settlement, causing increased crowding, heightened crime, and widespread illness. The wealthy and the middle classes from all districts also fled into the Settlement. Those who could afford to do so took flight from Shanghai to Hong Kong or to other distant cities protected from the Dwarf Bandits by the presence of British civilians and the British armed forces.

Life in the Chinese districts of Shanghai — in Chapei, Kiangwan, Pootung, Nantao, Woosung, Lungwha, and Huxi — was difficult. All lights were turned off every night from fear of air raids by the Kwantung or the KMT; inflation soared; and more and more Dwarf-Bandit troops poured into those districts every day, taking over large houses, hotels, and office buildings.

The Kwantung announced it would begin to exercise the policy it had used in Nanking known as *The Three Alls* — kill all, burn all, destroy all. This notification caused more and more people living in the outer districts to flee to the International Settlement. The overcrowding became desperately unhealthy.

Kwantung troops and tanks spent every day parading around the city — outside the treaty concessions — strutting about in columns of four, showing off their might and their implicit threat to the city and our population, sucking in and swallowing the city's spirit.

But not everyone took the Dwarf Bandit's posturing seriously.

In the Settlement, the Europeans and Americans who hadn't fled pretended they were not part of the melee going on all around them. Of course, that attitude did not stop them from complaining in their newspapers that the concessions had become overcrowded, filthy, and noisy, as swarms of frightened Shanghainese swept in from outside the Settlement's walls.

The British and Americans who had not yet fled the Settlement continued to think of themselves as special, as above the fray, protected by a century-old treaty that had created the concessions. Typically, the Round-Eyes only acknowledged the problems on those rare occasions when they took time away from their dinner parties to stand on balconies and rooftops, and passed around binoculars so they could watch flames lick across the northern parts of the city as the Kwantung set fire to buildings in the outer Chinese districts.

Outside the treaty concessions, every street corner was piled high with sandbags, behind which hovered ever-watching Dwarf-Bandit soldiers armed with mounted machine guns.

Tanks and other armored vehicles stood by in other areas, disdainfully keeping watch over the passing population.

Commerce in Chapei, Hongkew, and the other Chinese districts came to a standstill as shops and stalls were destroyed by fire, looted by soldiers, or permanently shuttered by their owners.

The outer districts exuded the sense of a time bomb ticking away, awaiting their eventual destruction.

CHAPTER 28

MEI-HUA AND ELI MADE ARRANGEMENTS to meet again. This time their rendezvous occurred in the dining room of the Medhurst Apartments/Hotel, a 12-story modern structure located at 934 Bubbling Well Road in the Settlement. The Medhurst was reputed to be a favorite meeting place for gangsters and warlords. The apartments/hotel boasted that its nightclub never closed, that its dining room served patrons until 3:00 a.m., and that its room service supplied guests with heroin or opium on request.

Mei-hua arrived with Bik in tow.

As Eli started to enter the building, he heard a loud, shrill buzzing tone from the street behind him. It was the *huan tou — the barber's tuning fork* — which was how barbers announced their arrival in a neighborhood so everyone who needed a haircut or shave could come outside, wait his turn in line, then sit on the small, triangular wooden barber's stool to be serviced.

Strange custom, Eli thought, as he remembered having his hair cut in Breslau in a well-appointed indoor shop having five barber's chairs. *I never will get used to having my hair cut out on the sidewalk with the whole neighborhood watching.*

He entered the dining room, saw Mei-hua seated at a small table. She was smoking a cigarette. He walked over.

"It's good to see you again," Mei-hua said. She kissed him on his cheek.

"I didn't know you have a dog," Eli said, as he pointed to Bik.

"She belongs to my comrade. I'm watching over her this week. Her name is Bik."

Eli leaned over and petted Bik.

They waited until the serving coolie had poured tea for them, filled their water glasses with ice water, set down the menus for them to read, and then left them alone.

"Everything is in place," Mei-hua said.

"Excellent. I will start the propaganda campaign with tomorrow's edition of *Slovo*," Eli said.

They spoke no more of this. They each knew their role and responsibility in carrying out the plan. There was no need to talk more of this in the restaurant among prying ears.

They ate a hearty meal, hugged each other as they said goodbye, then left the building, with Bik trotting close behind Mei-hua.

CHAPTER 29

ELI HAD BEEN PESTERING ME to let him help with the kidnapping investigation (although he did not yet know that this was what my new case concerned), but I wasn't quite ready to do that, not with his lack of experience. I couldn't take a chance on him because he still was untested in the field. I planned to let him occasionally come along with me to observe and learn, but only when his presence could not come back to cause me problems.

Eli had good powers of analysis, but that is not the same as knowing how to read people when you deal with them or how to read a new situation when you unexpectedly find yourself in it. That only comes slowly, often painfully, from the accumulation of knowledge gained from participating with people, as well as participating in various situations, sometimes successfully, sometimes not.

I did, however, have an idea how I could satisfy him for now and, perhaps, help me, too. I would give him a taste of a different lifestyle, one not likely to be known by a young Jewish immigrant.

I invited Eli to meet me in the French Concession at the *Heavenly Palace* — the Frenchtown nightclub owned by Elder Brother. The club is located at Avenue Edouard VII.

The club has been the perfect vehicle for Elder Brother's varied, but unrealized, criminal ambitions. It has brought him steady cash flow and good *joss*. The club has permitted Elder Brother to play the role of generous host and showman to Shanghai's underworld, a role he cherishes because it feeds his ego and fits in with his fantasy that he is a successful criminal, associating with others of like mind and desires.

This environment is the type of surroundings Eli will have to frequent if he works for me. This is the type milieu where, as a fledgling PI, he will meet and develop contacts who eventually will become his informants. I wanted him to get used to this type environment so he will be indifferent to the many distractions and temptations such surroundings offer to challenge a newcomer PI.

I arrived first and glanced around. Not much had changed since the last time I was here, seven or eight months ago. I don't come here often because, at Elder Brother's suggestion, we tend to get together in the Settlement at one of its nightclubs so Elder Brother can see what the competition might be doing that he can copy.

The club wasn't packed with customers yet. It still was too early in the evening for many of its regulars. But there was a small, somewhat smart-looking crowd of young men — triad gangsters, I assumed, from the look of their western-style suits — with comparatively-attired women hanging onto them.

There also were several attractive White-Russian and Chinese women, who were dressed in tight-fitting — slit on the side up-to-the-thigh — dresses called *chi-pai.* These women were sitting on folding chairs near the back of the room. They were taxi dancers who engaged in the most popular feature offered at the *Heavenly Palace.* They were waiting for customers — men or women — to invite them to dance to the music of this month's American *jazz band* that had been imported to the club by Elder Brother. Each taxi dance cost the customer the price of a ticket and a small bottle of Champagne for two.

What was unusual about Elder Brother's taxi dancers, and the reason they were so popular compared to the taxi-dancing women in other clubs, was that Elder Brother refused to follow the local custom that required that the dancers a club hired be either White Russian women or Chinese women, but not a mix of both, as they were at the *Heavenly Palace.*

Closer to where I stood sat the flower-seller girls who waited to take customers upstairs to pillow for an hour. These women all were White Russians.

Elder Brother was nowhere in sight, nor was he in his office when I went there to see him to say hello, just in case he had come in early tonight. He likely would be in later in the evening — around 11:00 p.m. — when the club was jumping and crowded, but after Eli and I will have left. That timing was his usual practice.

Eli arrived on time. I showed him around the club and explained the operation to him. As I suspected, this must have been his first experience in a French Concession nightclub since his eyes remained wide open the whole time we toured. His head swiveled continuously as attractive women passed by us, smiled at us, and often gave Eli the *Hello, Handsome, come to me with your pockets full of Yuan* look.

We settled in at a table in the corner, away from the dance

floor and the band. We ordered drinks. Eli never stopped looking over at the women sitting at the bar.

"*Ayeeyah"* I said. "First time in a nightclub?" I smiled. The answer was obvious.

He nodded, looked sheepishly at me, then furtively looked back at the bar. He looked back at me.

"Does it show?" he said.

"No. Not at all." I shook my head. "Just a guess."

Eli finished his drink and ordered another. I decided it was time to tell him one of the reasons I invited him to join me here.

"Eli," I said, as he reluctantly turned back to face me, "I didn't bring you here just so you could admire the flower-seller and taxi-dancing girls. I wanted you to see another side of Shanghai life that will be important for you to know if you become a PI. I also want to talk to you about my current investigation."

He sat up straighter and focused on me. I think he blushed, although I couldn't be sure under the dimmed lights. I would have blushed in his circumstance.

"The investigation? Are you finally going to let me help you?" he said.

"Yes and no. I'll explain."

He slumped slightly.

"What I mean is, no, you cannot do any investigating for me, out on your own. Not yet. You don't have any experience. But, yes, there is another way you might be able to help me."

"How am I supposed to become experienced if I'm not allowed to investigate because I don't have experience?"

"Experience will come later. Indirectly, bit by bit. I'll eventually let you investigate matters that will not have much adverse consequences if you mess up. And you will mess up sometime. Maybe more than once. We all do when we start out.

"Meantime, you will learn on easier, less important cases, not on the politically sensitive case I'm involved with now."

He seemed disappointed. He slumped further in his chair. "All right. How can I help you then?" he said.

"Based on the files I gave you to review and we talked about, I must say I admire your power of analysis, so I now want to take you to the next step. I will give you a specific problem to think about. I hope you'll see ways of approaching it I haven't seen."

"Here's the problem. A wealthy man is kidnapped. He is held somewhere for several weeks without any demand being made for ransom or other form of tribute. Nothing is demanded. Nothing is given. The man, however, offers payment to his abductors if they will free him, but they turn it down. They say they have no interest in his money. Then, a while later, they set him free. He was never harmed by them.

"What are the possible reasons this happened? Why would someone do that?"

CHAPTER 30

THE FIRST THING JMP INSPECTOR Detective Harue did after receiving his assignment from the Kwantung general was to order a member of his senior staff to organize and run the refugee-herding and intimidation tasks he and the general envisioned.

It did not take much of a genius, he decided, to frighten people so they would flee to, and then remain within, the Settlement's walls, under the protection of the Round-Eyes, then not leave the Settlement unless necessary or only temporarily.

He would devote himself to the other, but more worthy task. He would concentrate on rooting out Communist and KMT spies. This surely would bring him more favorable attention with the general than would herding groups of frightened Chinese into the International Settlement.

He began his espionage quest by assigning five members of his staff — all JMP constables — to the task of gathering information on civilians who were known to be, or who were suspected of being, active or former members of the KMT or the CCP.

When the list was ready, he assigned other, more experienced staff to investigate each person. One name turned up having affiliations with both the CCP and the KMT.

That was highly unusual, he thought.

That person was a young Chinese woman named Wu Meihua. Reportedly, she had once been very active in the CCP. Later, his staff told him, she renounced her membership in the Communist Party and became a KMT civilian worker at the Ministry of Justice. Her father was a KMT colonel.

Hai! Harue thought. *How odd she would have had membership in both political parties.*

Was she a double agent, a spy for the KMT and for the CCP, a spy who also would spy on the Kwantung during this period of relative truce between the two otherwise antagonistic Chinese parties?

He was sure this woman was a spy for someone. *But for whom? And was she a spy against the Kwantung army?*

He would have her watched. Then, when the time was right, he would arrest her and deport her to an internment camp where she eventually would be executed for espionage.

CHAPTER 31

I KNEW I COULD NOT TURN again to Sassoon for useful information. I believed he truly was baffled by the kidnapping and had nothing more to offer me. At least not now, not until or unless I could approach him with new information that might trigger his memory about additional details concerning the crime he hadn't yet considered.

I intended to meet with him from time-to-time to bring him up to date on my investigation, hopefully to give him some new information. I hoped this would pay off by refreshing his memory concerning some detail he'd forgotten or had never consciously thought about before.

I decided to approach the investigation from a different direction. I had requested copies of the SMP's files concerning the murder of Sir Victor's comprador. Normally, the SMP is reluctant to allow civilians (as I now am, thanks to Sassoon) to review its files while a case still is open. This was not true in this instance. The files were waiting for me at my office when I arrived there. In that regard, Sir Victor's power in Shanghai proved to be very helpful.

The chief inspector sent me carbon copies of the police reports, the coroner's report and the fingerprint reports. He also sent me black and white prints of the crime scene photos. I was told, via a note from the chief inspector that came with the package, that the Murder Book was not included since it could not be duplicated, but I was welcome to come to the central station to review it and take notes. He added that if I did come to the station house to look at it, I should come armed with a plausible excuse why I was doing so. Discretion, he reminded me, was absolutely necessary in this investigation. I decided to defer my review of the Murder Book for now, but I certainly would turn to it soon.

The most useful thing the chief inspector did was point me to the conclusions arrived at by the Special Branch inspector detectives who had investigated the homicide. They concluded that the comprador had not been murdered by someone working for a business rival of Sassoon. The SMP concluded, the report said, that the police could not determine a motive for the killing, but noted that when they tried to arrange an interview with the comprador's taipan — Sir Victor Sassoon — they were not able to meet with him for reasons not explained. The report noted, therefore, that for the time being the case was suspended as unsolved, and that the investigating inspector detectives considered Sir Victor to be a viable suspect in his comprador's murder. The SMP, the report stated, intended to activate the case again as soon as they were able to interview Sassoon.

If they only knew, I thought.

I spent a few hours reviewing the material Chapman sent over.

I first read the Incident Report completed by each constable and inspector detective who visited the crime scene. This is a report which is a simple, one-page form that notes the few facts and impressions that could be ascertained by observation, without further investigation. This report is always completed by the first constable or inspector detective to arrive at the crime scene.

The Incident Report then is expanded, using a one-sheet supplemental form, by all other constables and inspector detectives as they arrive and make their own observations. The supplemental form is supposed to be completed by each officer based on his own observations, without prior discussion with other cops who had been there ahead of him, and without reference to the Incident Report or other supplemental forms filled out by other arriving policemen. The theory is that one or more of the supplementals might suggest fresh information based on fresh observations, untainted by previous reports. It rarely works out that way. In practice, most, if not all, SMP constables and inspector detectives fill out their supplemental forms later when they are back at the station house, tainted by their earlier discussions with other constables and inspector detectives while at the crime scene.

The black and white crime scene photographs — there were eleven of them — were each made from a different angle as the photographer, using his 5x7 format Speed Graphic press camera and flash, circled the body, taking a picture every few steps. At the end of the process, the body was photographed at 360 degrees.

The photographs showed exactly what the constable who was first on the scene had described in his Incident Report, and what the other coppers described in their supplemental forms.

In the photographs, the comprador was sprawled on his back on the sidewalk in front of *Wing On*. He had one arm askew, at an improbable right angle to his side. I could see two bloody, black and white entrance wounds where the comprador had been shot in the chest. The photos did not prove helpful to me.

I next read through the coroner's report, slowly going over its details, mindful how such reports always reduce the victim, and, therefore, human life to centimeters and grams. The first statement in the comprador's report set the tone, describing the victim as a male Celestial who measured a certain number of centimeters and weighed a certain number of grams. Nothing in thc rcport seemed useful.

In the end, the materials sent to me by the chief inspector proved to be a dead end as far as my investigation of Sassoon's kidnapping was concerned. The materials might eventually be helpful in solving the comprador's murder, but for now they offered me no clues who kidnapped Sir Victor or why they might have done so.

But my time with the murder file hadn't been entirely wasted.

Now that I had some grasp of the dual-purpose crime scene, I again reviewed what little I'd learned from talking with Sir Victor. This gave me a sequence of events. Not much, but some. Unfortunately, this, too, did not help much.

But I wasn't discouraged by this condition. I had learned years ago, while still a SMP Special Branch inspector detective, that even though I often needed to know the sequence of events to understand a crime, having that sequence did not necessarily suggest or prove causality. In this investigation, I did not see in the SMP's files or among the notes I made when I interviewed Sassoon, any clues even suggesting causality. I needed more information. For now, Sir Victor was a dry well, not much help to me.

I left my office and rode an electric streetcar to Frenchtown and, afterward, to Chapei. I located and spoke with several of the paid informants I use from time-to-time. All were associated with the Green Gang or with other criminal triads; all had their own connections and informants throughout the city. All operated as criminals on a day-to-day basis.

I'd learned over time that a private investigator could barely succeed in Shanghai if he did not pay attention to gossip, which was the common language of the Shanghainese and expatriate communities. In this city, it generally isn't science that solves our crime cases, it is rumor and gossip. The recently conceived science known as forensics is useful to convict criminals once we've identified them, but cases in Shanghai are frequently solved because people love to talk, even when it is against their best interest to do so. Fortunately, my flock of informants loves to listen, and thereafter talk to me, and to be well-paid by me for doing so.

I learned through experience to rely on my informants to breathe fresh air into my investigations when I stalled or, sometimes, when I had never even gotten started on my own. They would hear rumors no one would ever talk to me about, and would bring me those several bits of information so I could piece the scraps together into one unified whole or could use them to lead me to other facts.

The informants' reliability inevitably varied. It depended on the information I needed, the reward I offered for it, and, of course, their unstated self-interest or agenda at the time I sought the information. On this occasion I was prepared to pay very well because I could recover my payments from Sassoon as an expense of the investigation.

Without describing the kidnapping to any of them, I turned the informants loose to see if they could learn of any small-talk concerning a recent crime against a well-placed, wealthy, Shanghai Round-Eyes resident.

One by one, over the next few days, my informants reported back to me. They'd turned up nothing. No gossip. No eye witnesses to a crime such as I alluded to (other than the murder of the comprador which, they each said, did not seem to fit the crime I'd vaguely described). No potential suspects. Indeed, no information that a crime had even been committed against a person such as I had described to them.

Since I had nothing new to go on, I asked myself the basic questions concerning all investigations: who had access to the victim; who had motive to commit the crime; and, who had the opportunity and means to do so.

This concept of an investigation was similar to the beginning of an archaeological dig. This was an image that often occurred to me as I started an investigation — uncovering the hidden pieces of the crime, laying them out to organize and understand individually, then seeking to understand them as a group, and finally fitting the pieces together, searching for patterns.

I thought about Sassoon's case. I focused on the classic techniques used by the police and by private investigators to inquire into major crimes — paying attention to the crime scene (I could not do that in this instance), interviewing participants and witnesses (there were none other than Sir Victor), and learning about the victim's life and relationships — friends, love relationships, enemies, criminal connections, criminal record, known bad habits, marriage or marriages, divorces, business conflicts, debts, and financial issues.

This sounded straight-forward, almost easy, but it wasn't. Too much of this technique relied on the good faith participation of people who were tangentially involved — the victims (whose bodies and histories might or might not yield valuable information), participants in the crime, and witnesses (there were none in this instance) — all who needed to be cooperative if they were going to be useful.

I did not yet have enough information to begin to formulate a loose hypothesis that would guide my search for other evidence. None of the usual, clear, understood rules for investigating a crime was there.

I had come to a dead end before I'd barely begun.

CHAPTER 32

Pock-Marked Huang's men watched Mei-hua for eight days and nights. Then Huang reported to Big-Eared Tu with new information he believed would interest him.

As always, they met in Tu's Great Room.

"I believe the woman we spoke about, the one who was a CCP member before she took a job with the KMT, is a spy for the CCP. Her KMT-colonel father acts as her cover, depicting her as now loyal to Chiang."

"Is her father also involved in her treachery?"

"It doesn't seem so. It appears he is her dupe."

"Eliminate her. Don't waste any more time with her. That will be one less insect to be concerned with. Make it appear to be an accident of war so we do not jeopardize the delicate truce existing between that vermin Mao and Generalissimo Chiang. No one will know the difference."

"Perhaps, Master Tu, you will change your mind when I tell you another piece of information we just learned about her," Huang said. "In the course of our surveillance of this woman, we learned she has a lover who you know well."

"And who is that?" Tu said. He frowned and tapped his finger against the side of his chair. He felt Huang was stringing him along, trying to make him beg for information that Huang should have immediately offered.

It is a dangerous game for Huang to be playing with me, Tu thought.

"Her lover is Ling Sun-jin, the disgraced former policeman, now a private investigator."

Tu smiled. All was forgiven. This could be valuable information for him to tuck away in the deep folds of his Mandarin gown. He looked into Huang's eyes.

"Most interesting, my friend," Tu said.

"Should I still eliminate the woman, and, perhaps, the ex-policeman also, Master Tu?"

Tu shook his head. "Perhaps later. Perhaps both of them. For now, keep watch over her. At some point, I might wish to question her."

CHAPTER 33

ELI HAD NOT YET GOTTEN back to me concerning the kidnapping situation I'd given him to think about, yet he again had been pestering me to teach him the private investigator's business. I was beginning to think he might be nothing more than a talker who wanted to be spoon-fed information, but who wasn't prepared to do the hard work necessary to learn the business. I invited him to meet me at my office. I would put the question directly to him and see what I thought of his response.

I noticed when Eli entered my office he looked at Bik, and seemed surprised to see her.

"I didn't know you have a dog," he said. "What's its name?"

"Bik. She lives with me, but sometimes lives with my girlfriend."

Girlfriend? Sun-jin and Mei-hua are boyfriend and girlfriend? That's interesting. I wonder why neither ever mentioned the other to me?

We sat at opposite ends of a wooden bench I kept for informal meetings with clients. We each held a bottle of *Clover* beer in our hand as we faced each other.

"Have you thought about the problem I gave you?" I said.

Eli looked down at his lap and slightly slumped in his chair.

"*Oy vey! — Oh, no!* I've thought a lot about it, but haven't gotten anywhere. It's actually been driving me crazy. I think about it all the time, but cannot come up with any possibilities. It's the strangest problem I can imagine."

He looked away from me and stared at the beer bottle in his hand. Then he slowly turned back to me.

"That's why I've avoided saying anything to you about it." He stared at the floor as he admitted this . "I'm embarrassed and angry at myself."

I liked his candor. I smiled. This was the first time I'd heard this Jewish immigrant use a Yiddish phrase, as his father often did when he spoke with me. I was surprised since, according to his father, Eli wanted to assimilate into our Chinese culture as quickly as possible. Perhaps that slip reflected his frustration with the problem I'd given him.

"*Ayeeyah!* Relax, Eli. Things are not as bad as you might think. It's not a problem I made up. It's the case I am currently struggling with.

"I haven't been able to figure this out either," I said. "I was hoping with your fresh eyes you might suggest something I haven't thought about. It's obvious we both have some work to do on it."

I could see him relax. "It's a real case? Not just a situation you made-up to test me?"

"It's real, and I think eventually we will solve it."

"We? He smiled. "You said, we."

"Yes, I did. We," I said, again for his benefit.

I liked his response so I put aside my suspicion that he'd been lazy. I decided to find some way he could help me with Sassoon's case.

"You can come along with me as I pursue the investigation.

We can talk about it and see if together we can come up with an answer. This, along with keeping your eyes and ears open, paying attention to what I do and do not do, and asking questions when we're alone, will teach you much about the business of being a PI."

I watched Eli suddenly frown. He looked at me with what can only be described as suspicion.

"Why did you change your mind? You said before you didn't have time to teach me."

"True, but circumstances have changed. I'm under pressure to wrap up this case, but I haven't made much headway. I can use your viewpoint, even your naïve questions. They might trigger an idea for me I haven't thought about. At this point, I'll take all the help and any good *joss* I can get."

CHAPTER 34

THE CHAIRMAN OF *WING ON* met with me in his office. I brought Eli along with me.

"Thank you, sir, for taking the time to meet with us," I said. "I'll try to be brief because I know you're a busy man."

"How can I help you, Mr. Ling?" He ignored Eli.

"I have a letter here from Sir Victor Sassoon asking that you tell me everything I might want to know concerning his meeting with you several weeks ago. Although I am helping Sir Victor with an unrelated private matter, your meeting with him might be relevant to that inquiry because of its timing."

"What do you want to know?"

"Sir Victor told me he met with you to discuss the possibility that his company might buy this property. Is that correct?"

"It is."

"Were you interested?" I recalled what Sir Victor had told me. I wanted to see if Sir Victor had correctly interpreted the president's response.

"I am interested. Subject, of course, to my review of relevant financial information and to other, substantive business terms I proposed to him. Sir Victor had no problem with my questions and proposal. He said he would gather the relevant financial information for me and bring it to our next meeting ."

That certainly was at odds with what Sassoon told me.

"So you tentatively were interested in his project?"

"As I said, I was. I still am. Especially if he agrees to the non-financial terms I suggested to him."

"Would you tell me what those were?"

He seemed uncomfortable with that thought so I reminded him of what Sir Victor had requested in his letter I brought with me.

He nodded. "Well, price and payment terms, of course. And, I wanted to be a silent partner in the new hotel he would erect on this site. He agreed with that. I also wanted him to be a silent partner in the new *Wing On* department store we would erect somewhere else in the Settlement to replace this one. He agreed in principle with that concept, too."

"Was his comprador with him when you met?"

"No. Just me and Sir Victor. Although I understand his comprador later was coming to deliver the financials to me when he was killed outside the store. I didn't see him, myself. My secretary took the package from him to give to me."

"What's the current status of Sir Victor's project? Are you still a part of it?"

"It's on hold. Everything came to a halt when Sir Victor's comprador was murdered and Sir Victor disappeared for several weeks. I haven't heard anything about the project since my meeting with Sir Victor."

I looked at my notebook to see if I'd missed any questions I wanted to ask. I hadn't."

I stood up. "Thank you, sir, for your time. I appreciate it."

We leaned across the desk toward each other and shook hands. He nodded at Eli. I also bowed slightly. Then we left.

Unless my memory had been faulty, and I don't think it was, Sir Victor's account of the meeting and *Wing On*'s president's account were exactly the opposite of each other's. One of those men had lied to me.

CHAPTER 35

Akio Harue sat in his office rereading the report he'd received from the staff member who had been following Mei-hua. Nothing in it suggested she was a spy. Yet his intuition, his experience with the Chinese, and his investigatory instincts told him that this woman, who had been a member of the CCP, but now worked for the KMT, must be spying for one or the other, or for both, against each other.

Hai! Perhaps she is a double agent working for both sides and against both, he thought. *If that is true, it is likely she also is spying on the Kwantung army.*

He read again the most startling information in the report. This woman was having a relationship with the former SMP Special Branch inspector detective, Ling Sun-jin.

He shook his head abruptly. *This is most interesting.* He smiled a wolfish smile.

He thought about the bad blood that existed between him and the former SMP inspector detective. It had started during the investigation of the flower-seller girls murders, and continued afterward so it infected the investigation of the homicide of the Japanese-national nightclub singer, the woman known as the Golden Swan. He smiled again, his smile more rapacious than before.

Harue put down the report. He yelled to his JMP staff sergeant sitting at the desk outside his door, "Send two constables to me. I have an assignment for them."

Two JMP constables stepped up to me as I walked out of my office. It was clear they'd been waiting for me to appear on Bubbling Well Road. They insisted I come with them to JMP headquarters in Hongkew. They threatened me with arrest if I resisted.

"You don't have jurisdiction in the Settlement," I said. "You can't arrest me."

"*Hai!* We will take you with us, one way or the other, and sort out jurisdiction another time."

I nodded my reluctant assent to go with them.

They would not tell me why we were going to JMP headquarters in Hongkew or who I would meet with. I was furious.

"Why have you brought me here?" I said to Harue, once I'd been led into his office. "I haven't committed any crime. Certainly not in any district over which the JMP or you have jurisdiction. I intend to report your actions. This is tantamount to kidnapping me."

"Sit down, Mr. Ling," Harue said, as he pointed to a chair near his desk. "There's more to this than the JMP," Harue said. "I also work for the Kwantung. You are here because I have good reason to believe you are a spy acting against the Kwantung."

I shook my head and tried not to laugh. "That's nonsense. I'm not a spy. Not for anyone. I'm a private investigator."

"You are a spy for the KMT. The only question is, who are you spying against? The CCP? The British? The Americans? Us? All of us?"

"I'm not a spy. Why would you even think that?"

"You work with your lover, Wu Mei-hua, to spy. We know all about her, and about the two of you."

"What are you talking about, Harue?" I could feel my face growing hot and my back becoming rigid as I listened to this fool.

"Your girlfriend, she was an open member of the CCP, and now she works for the KMT. Don't you find that unnatural?" he said.

"Not at all. She had a change of heart, saw the evil that the CCP represents, publicly renounced the CCP, and took a job with the KMT. She has to earn a living. I don't see anything strange about that."

"I believe she is a spy for the CCP, perhaps also for the KMT, and that you are, too. Otherwise, you would not be associated with her. It's just a matter of catching one of you, or both, in the act. Then I will arrest you both."

"Why are you doing this?"

"You and your girlfriend are untrustworthy, like all Chinese," Harue said. He looked hard at me, and smirked.

"You don't accept how benevolent we Japanese are acting in trying to lift you up from your backward condition by helping China save itself from itself.

"If only you would recognize our superiority and tutelage, we could permit you to govern yourself, with our indirect help and loyal personnel, of course."

I decided that silence was the best response, so I said

nothing. There was nothing I could say or argue that would counter Harue's arrogance.

"In the meantime, you now are officially prohibited from pursuing your investigations in any of the areas of Shanghai occupied by the Kwantung army. In fact, starting now, those areas are off limits for you in all respects, personal or business. If I find you disobeying this order, I will arrest you and ship you to an internment camp for re-education."

"*Ayeeyah!* You can't do that. You are banning me from going home. I live in Chapei. The Kwantung is all over that district."

"You are advised to follow my order, Mr. Ling."

CHAPTER 36

Mei-hua left her office and walked toward the trolley stand to ride the streetcar to a stop near her flat in Frenchtown. She boarded the third trolly to approach her, the first two being reserved for Kwantung soldiers.

The streets echoed with the clanging of distant streetcar bells and the screech of metal wheels on metal tracks, the bellowing of automobile horns, and the incessant piercing shrieks of the coolie rickshaw pullers. Ironically, the quietest sources of all the noise — and they were not a quiet source at all, except by comparison — were the many hucksters who shouted at her as she walked by them in their effort to pull Mei-hua, and any other passerby, into their stalls to buy their wares.

Mei-hua stood on the corner, along with other pedestrians, waiting for the orange-turbaned Sikh to wave her and the others across the street. Suddenly, a black Buick automobile pulled to the curb, its tires screeching. The back door of the vehicle abruptly opened and two men climbed out. They fixed their eyes on Mei-hua, then briskly strode over to her. They silently placed themselves on either side of her, crowding her.

"Wu Mei-hua," one of the men said, not as a question, but

as a statement meant to arrest her attention, "please come with us. We mean you no harm." He canted his head toward the curbed automobile.

Mei-hua dropped the package she carried and assumed a *Shaolin* attack position, ready to strike at the first sign either man meant to touch her.

"Please relax. We, too, are skilled in the ways of *Shaolin*," said one of the men. "If you attack us, it will not be a fair fight. Together we will cause you much damage."

As he said this, he stepped back, moving several meters away. The other man did the same.

Mei-hua relaxed. "What do you want?" she said, speaking *Hu*. "Where do you intend to take me?"

"To meet with our boss, Master Tu."

What could Big-Eared Tu possibly want with me? she wondered. She nodded, picked up her package, and followed the men to the car.

"You honor me, Miss Wu, by accepting my invitation to visit with me," Big-Eared Tu said.

As if I had any choice. "The honor is mine, Master Tu." Mei-hua slightly bowed her head to show respect.

Although Mei-hua was eager to find out why she'd been summoned to Tu's home, she knew that Confucian custom and Taoist decorum required that she not directly inquire of him, that established obligations of propriety and respect required that she permit Tu to ramble on about other matters until he was ready to enlighten her.

"Permit me to show you some of my most esteemed scholars' artifacts," Tu said. He stood up and smiled at Mei-hua.

"Thank you, Uncle," she said, employing the proper term that younger Chinese men and women used to address older Chinese men they had not met before.

Tu led Mei-hua across the Great Room to a huanghuali-wood table sitting beneath two hanging cages made from beautiful, intricately woven bamboo. One cage had songbirds within its confines; the other cage was populated with Tu's lucky crickets.

Tu gestured toward the table. "These scholars' artifacts are among my most prized possessions," he said, as he pointed to seven decorated ink stones, an array of calligraphy brushes, an elm brush pot, a seal box, and a small, limestone Bodhisattva head sitting on a stone bed of lotus leaves.

When they finished admiring his objects, Tu said, "Permit me to serve you tea, Miss Wu." He pointed to a nearby red lacquer low table having a tea pot and two blue and white porcelain sipping bowls on it.

Tu sat on a silk pillow on one side of the table. Mei-hua sat on a similar pillow across from him. They slurped their tea without speaking.

When a servant had cleared the table and replaced the teapot with Tu's small opium pipe — which Tu immediately proceeded to light — Tu said, "I know who you are and what you are. I know you work for the KMT in the Ministry of Justice. I also know you are a spy for the CCP."

Mei-hua's spine stiffened. Her throat tightened. She slowly shook her head and said, speaking as softly as Tu had spoken, "*Bù! — No!* You are wrong, Master Tu. I am just a lowly clerk, not a spy." She bit her lip.

"And your friend, Ling Sun-jin," Tu said, "I know he also is a spy for the enemy?"

One hour later, Mei-hua and Eli met in front of the Vienna Garden Restaurant on Majestic Road. They did not go inside. Instead, they walked toward the Bund so they could mingle with the mid-day crowd, and not seem suspicious as they talked. Mei-hua was certain Big-Eared Tu had arranged to have her followed.

She described her meeting with Tu.

"He said he will cause me great harm if I continue assisting the CCP by causing spies to infiltrate the KMT. Perhaps he will even kill me," Mei-hua said.

How does he know?" Eli said. "He's guessing. He does not know anything about what we do."

"Big-Eared Tu is said to know everything that goes on in Shanghai," Mei-hua said. She stared briefly at the ground, then glanced around to see if they were being watched.

"Should we abort our mission?" Eli said.

"No."

"Then what? I do not want to see you murdered by Tu's thugs."

"It is time," Mei-hua said, that we bring my friend, Sun-jin, into our mission. He will be displeased I have deceived him, that you and I are assisting the CCP, but he also will forgive us once I have introduced you to him and explain that we have been working together. Sun-jin will offer us pragmatic, good advice."

Eli blushed. "Sun-jin and I already know each another. I have been learning from him how to become a PI."

"You do?" Mai-hua said. She frowned. "Tell me about that."

CHAPTER 37

I SET UP A MEETING WITH the chief inspector. I wanted to ask him a few questions, to clarify some points concerning the investigation. I decided to take Eli with me as part of his training.

⸻

When we arrived, the chief inspector came out of his office to greet me. He glanced over at Eli, then faced me and glared at me. I introduced Eli to him as my colleague.

"Very nice to meet you, young man," Chapman said. He turned to face me.

"Sorry, Old Boy, but only you may meet with me. This investigation still is confidential even though it now is being pursued by Sir Victor, not the SMP. The reasons originally underlying confidentiality remain the same. Nothing has changed that."

He faced Eli again. "It isn't personal, young man."

"But—" I said.

"No *but,* Sun-jin. If you want to talk to me about your investigation, come in alone. Otherwise, I have work to do."

I followed Chapman into his office.

CHAPTER 38

LATER THAT SAME EVENING I joined Mei-hua for our dinner meal. We met at the *Yellow Dragon Inn* on Chun Shi Road in the Settlement.

"You remember the Dwarf Bandit Harue who is an inspector detective with the JMP?" I said, after we sat down at our table. "He now is also working for the Kwangtung. Apparently he is a civil officer in the Dwarf Bandits' army.

"He recently confronted me and told me I'm only permitted to investigate a crime in the Settlement and in Frenchtown. Obviously, that's not convenient if the evidence leads me toward Chapei, Hongkew or elsewhere. He also told me I'm not permitted to visit districts outside the two concessions, not even for personal reasons, not even to go home."

Mei-hua shook her head and laughed. "I doubt you'll be influenced by Harue," she said, "so please take care when you enter prohibited districts. I worry about you when you decide to defy authority."

"Here's something else," I said. "He told me he thinks you're a spy for the KMT. Actually, he said he thinks we both are spies."

Mei-hua shrugged and rolled her eyes. "I'm not. Are you?"

I know I'm not, I thought, *but I don't know about you. I sometimes wonder if you still maintain your ties to the CCP.*

I did not say this, although the possibility, because of her CCP history, made me wonder. I had never heard of any active Communist who actually cast aside his beliefs when he gave up his membership in the Party. Recanting ones belief in the CCP usually was a matter of convenience or outside pressure, not personal conviction.

"I have to figure out how to deal with him," I said. "He could become a problem for me as I investigate Sassoon's case."

Mei-hua nodded. She paused, then said, "I have some news of my own to tell you."

I looked at her expectantly. She briefly looked down at her tea bowl, then back up at me.

"I had a meeting today with Big-Eared Tu."

"Why would you do that?"

"Not voluntarily. He had me picked up on a street corner by two goons, then taken to him at his home. No one asked my permission."

"Tu abducted you? Forced you to meet with him?" I was furious. Angry at Tu's audacious act and angry at myself because I felt helpless to protect her in this situation, whatever it amounted to.

"Once I realized Tu had no interest in harming me, I became more curious than frightened or angry."

"What did he want?"

"Believe it or not, like Harue, Tu also thinks I'm a CCP spy. He warned me to cease that activity."

That stopped me. "That could be a problem, Mei-hua. Tu is anti-Communist, and is deeply embedded with Chiang and the KMT. Did he say why he thinks you're a spy?"

"No, but probably because of my history with the CCP. He said he does not believe my repudiation letter to the *North-China Daily News*. He thinks I now work for the KMT as a CCP mole."

"Maybe you should quit your KMT job," I said. "That would be the safe step to take."

"That is not going to happen. I like my job."

"I'm worried about you, Mei-hua."

"Don't waste your time. Instead, you should worry about yourself. Tu also thinks you're a spy," she said.

CHAPTER 39

I DECIDED TO TALK WITH ONE other informant. I had not been able to contact him before, although I had tried. This man was not a member of the Green Gang or a member of any other triad. He was a Dwarf Bandit who lived and worked in Hongkew. At the request of Avram Ben-David Rueben, I had done a favor for him, almost one year before, by getting his youngest son out of a serious gambling jam he'd gotten himself into with the Green Gang. To do this, I had called in some favors through Elder Brother. I did not charge him a fee for my services, also a favor by me to Avram.

The Dwarf Bandit has been a loyal informant ever since then. But now? While our countries are at war? I wondered if I could rely on him. I hoped when he realized my request was unrelated to anything military or to the war, he'd still help me.

I telephoned him at his place of work, using a code we'd set up to speak. He reluctantly agreed to see me. I also told him to expect to meet my colleague who would be with me. I didn't want him to bolt when he saw Eli with me.

I explained to Eli the many inconveniences and ensuing danger we might encounter from Dwarf Bandits and from Japanese residents of Hongkew. I also told him about Harue's order to me to stay out of the districts, which included Hongkew.

"If Harue arrests me for entering Hongkew, it could mean trouble for you, too, since you would be with me," I said.

"I experience problems every day in Hongkew from the local Dwarf Bandits, just going to and from my home in Little Vienna," he said. "I can handle myself."

We walked across the Public Gardens and crossed the Garden Bridge without incident, although we did have to show our papers on the bridge and had to bow to, as well as greet, the soldiers who inspected them.

As we entered Hongkew, I saw Dwarf Bandit civilians eyeing us. Some carried clubs. They watched us, it seemed to me, with great contempt in their eyes, but no one made any move to threaten or harm us.

Hongkew was even more congested than the areas across the river near the Bund. The streets were narrow, were tightly packed with low buildings, and with various vendors' stalls. The sidewalks were blocked by beggars seeking aid and by pedestrians standing in the middle of the sidewalk talking as loudly as they could so as to be heard over the *jenao — the general din and cacophony of the city* that gives Shanghai its vitality — and by aggressive groups of Kwantung soldiers who forced their way along the sidewalk, pushing aside young and old as they moved through the crowd.

As we walked on to meet our informant, we saw many lines of civilians, baskets in hand, waiting to receive their weekly food allowances.

We got together with my informant at the *Eight Imponderables*

Tea House on Rue du Roi. He worked there as the Number-One Boy.

Eli and I settled into a back corner. Our informant brought us a pot of tea. He eyed Eli with suspicion.

"This is my colleague," I said, nodding my head toward Eli. "You can trust him as you would me."

I explained what I needed from him. He promised to ask around and get back to me. I had no idea if his Dwarf Bandit heritage would play some role in undermining his willingness to help me. He might have felt he'd already paid his debt to me, but like most Dwarf Bandits I've dealt with, would not say no to another person or would not give them news they did not want to hear. That was a frustrating aspect of dealing with Dwarf Bandits, even potentially friendly ones. But he did have one advantage over my other informants. His contacts were in the Dwarf-Bandit community. My other informants could not enter that crowd to make inquiries.

After this meeting, I went home. Eli, since he already was in Hongkew, headed for his father's house.

CHAPTER 40

THE FOLLOWING MORNING, ELI CALLED and asked me to meet with him about an important matter. He wouldn't tell me what it concerned when I asked him.

We met at my office. Mei-hua entered with him. I was surprised. I didn't know they knew each other, but obviously they did.

"What is this?" I said, looking first at Mei-hua, then at Eli. "You know each other?"

They nodded.

"We know each other from our time as members of the CCP," Mei-hua said. "I was Eli's handler and mentor."

"You never told me, yet you both had dealings with me?" I said, my anger rising.

"You deceived me," I said, looking first at Mei-hua, then at Eli. "You made me seem a fool as I went about my business and personal dealings with each of you, while all along you acted together behind my back." I could feel my face and neck growing hot.

"It wasn't like that, Sun-jin," Eli said. "I never knew you and Mei-hua knew each other until I recently saw Bik with Mei-hua, then a few days later, I saw you with Bik. I immediately told Mei-hua."

"But not me. You didn't tell me."

"*Ayeeyah!* Sun-jin," Mei-hua said. "I never knew you know Eli because it never came up. There was no reason for it to have come up between us.

"Do I now have to give you a list of all the people I know to see if you also know them? Will you also give me such a list of your acquaintances? To what purpose?"

I shook my head. I wasn't sure what I felt. My instincts argued for anger, suggesting I'd been deceived, but my experience with Mei-hua and, recently, with Eli suggested this situation had just been a coincidence, with no malice meant. *Anyway,* I thought, *what difference does it make. We all now know we know one another.*

"I apologize to you, Sun-jin, but Eli and I did not intend to deceive or mislead you. We were just as uninformed as you were about our relationships. As soon as we realized the situation, we came here to tell you."

This made sense. I really couldn't justify remaining angry with them, so I purged the feeling.

"Are you both still active in the CCP?" I asked. I watched Mei-hua carefully. This would be a moment when I would have to decide if I could trust her or not, whether I will still want to cast my life with her.

Mei-hua and Eli glanced at each another, then looked at me.

"I still am active," Eli said. "I continue to work as the editor of *Slovo*, but you already know that."

"I, too, have remained active," Mei-hua said, "but secretly. I still have my father to contend with."

"And your previous disavowal of the Party and all it stands for?" I asked. "Did that not mean anything to you?"

"I engaged in that solely for the benefit of my parents, especially my father, who believes I have hurt his career in the KMT."

That was pretty much what I expected her to say.

"How active are you now, Mei-hua? And you, Eli? Anything for you beyond *Slovo*?" I said, as I turned to face him.

"We both are very active," Mei-hua said. "It is a function of the current state of war. We are implementing a plan to infiltrate Party members into KMT's bureaucracy at all levels. Everyone has been given his assignment. The process is unfolding as we speak," she said.

I had mixed feelings about this. I loved Mei-hua and liked Eli, but my loyalty was to China, to the Republic, and to the KMT. Yet I did not want to see any harm come to either Mei-hua or Eli because of me. I would have to navigate this situation carefully.

"The important thing now," I said, "is to protect you, Mei-hua, from Tu. He knows — or he thinks he knows — you are a spy. Tu will take action against you if we are not careful."

I looked at Eli. "I doubt Tu knows you also are a spy, or that he's even heard of you. You should be all right if you keep a low profile."

I looked back at Mei-hua who had stood up.

"We must convincingly demonstrate to Tu that you have ceased this reckless mission of yours, and also must convince him that you will not again engage in activities against Chiang and the KMT. That is your only path to forgiveness by him. I don't know if we can even achieve this."

"I will not do that, Sun-jin. I cannot do that. I would rather die at Tu's hand than turn my back on my country."

"China is your country," I said, "not the CCP."

"China and the CCP are inseparable as far as I'm concerned," she said. "For me, they are the Celestial *Yin* and *Yang*."

CHAPTER 41

I SPENT A RESTLESS NIGHT ALONE after my meeting with Mei-hua and Eli. I'd told Mei-hua I had to absorb the enormity of what she'd disclosed to me about her continuing Communist activity, and that the best way for me to do this was to think about it for a while. I slept alone, except for Bik, who, as always when she was at home, slept at the foot of my bed.

In the morning, I called Sassoon to set up another meeting. It took some doing because he seemed to be avoiding me, not taking or returning my calls. Then, just before noon, he called back and agreed to see me.

He greeted me coldly when I entered his office.

"You continue to waste time, Mr. Ling. We don't need to meet again. This should have been avoided." He blew out a cloud of dark cigar smoke.

"This is the final time," he said, "I will indulge your strange desire to review your lack of progress for me. After today, we will not meet again until you have something positive to report. And that better be soon." He stubbed out his cigar in his heavy, amber-color glass ashtray.

"I've already told you everything I know," he said. "You should be out investigating my kidnapping. That's what I'm paying you for."

I was losing patience with Sassoon. He continually pushed me to get results for him, but has been reluctant to cooperate with me. He's been a begrudging witness, at best. It was time for us to decide and deal with one question: Was Sir Victor running the investigation or was I? The answer obviously would have important consequences for me.

He hadn't offered me a seat when I entered his office, although he continued to sit behind his desk, so I pulled back a chair and sat down without his invitation.

"Sir Victor," I said, "these meetings we've had the past few days are part of my investigation." I made sure my voice conveyed my annoyance.

"If you want to run the investigation, do so. Or, if all you want to do is criticize the way I'm running it, do so. In either case, I'm out then. We either do it my way or I'm through."

I knew the risk I'd undertaken with this statement — immediate and long term — but I did not see any other course for me to take. I hoped my gambit would work.

Sassoon crossed his arms and tapped his foot. He glared at me. "Very well, then. Get on with it," he said, his impatience, and, perhaps, shock, evident. "It's your investigation."

"I don't intend to give you a progress report today. That's not why I'm here. Instead, I want to explain my methodology to you so you'll see what we're up against in this investigation."

Sir Victor stared at me, silently. His face and neck had become slightly crimson.

"I've investigated the kidnapping as I would investigate any case. I've studied the police reports, the coroner's report, the laboratory reports, and the crime scene photos concerning the murder of your comprador, hoping to find a lead, as part of that case — a lead that had been missed by the SMP because the SMP inspector detectives did not know they were looking into two crimes, not one. These all were dead ends.

"I've had my usual informants make inquiries, but that turned up nothing. I've interviewed the only relevant witness — you, Sir Victor — but you have not been able to help me." I paused to see what he would say about that.

"Correct. I've told you everything I know."

"There's one more thing, Sir Victor. I met with the president of *Wing On*. He claimed he was in favor of participating in a sale of his property to you, provided certain conditions were met. He said he only awaited information from you to move forward, information your comprador delivered to him the day he died."

I paused to see if Sir Victor reacted. He did not.

"Either he lied to me, sir, or you did."

Sassoon didn't respond. He made no attempt to justify his previous story that the president of *Wing On* had dismissed his offer to buy the department store's real estate. It was as if he'd never said it to me.

I let this pass (although I filed it away in my memory) because I had a more important point to make.

"I've given the crime a great deal of thought." I paused, looked hard into his eyes, and said, "Now it's time for you to come clean for me."

"What are you talking about?"

"I'm saying, Sir Victor, that it's time for you to be candid with me, to admit the truth to me. Otherwise we really are wasting our time."

"Are you suggesting I lied to you, that—"

"I'm suggesting I expect the complete truth from you, right now, without regard to what you might have told me before, or I am finished with this investigation."

Sir Victor raised one eyebrow and cast a glassy stare at me. He clenched his jaw and retrieved another cigar from his humidor.

I decided to take the initiative while he prepared to light his cigar.

"This isn't my first investigation, Sir Victor. So I find it curious there were no witnesses on Nanking Road in late morning who saw you being kidnapped. No police report of the kidnapping. No ransom or other demand from the kidnappers.

"I find it unlikely you were rebuffed in your attempts to pay a steep ransom for your release, and that you eventually were set free without any explanation."

I paused to see his reaction. He said nothing, so I continued.

"And I find it most strange that the case was kept secret, and then closed by the SMP after so short an investigation."

Sassoon finally spoke.

"It has been kept secret to protect my business interests, and the interests of my partners and investors."

"I don't believe that," I said. "That might have been relevant while you still were missing," I said, "but not now that you're back." I paused to let him respond, but he said nothing.

"All we have is your word you were snatched off a busy street in the middle of the morning, with no one around to notice. Don't you find it curious that no one came forward to report the event to the police?" I paused, then said, "I do."

Again, he said nothing.

After almost one full minute of strained silence, Sir Victor nodded and finally spoke.

"Okay. Have it your way."

He paused, then said, "You're instincts are correct. I wasn't kidnapped. I made up the whole thing."

CHAPTER 42

"AYEEYAH," I SAID. I WAS shocked. I never expected that. "Made the whole thing up? Why?"

I didn't know if I was happy or not he'd admitted this to me.

On the one hand, in the face of that admission, I wanted to close the file, collect my fee for the time and effort I'd put into his phony case, and get on with my regular PI business.

On the other hand, I was furious for having wasted my time and for him having dealt out abuse to me every time I reported my lack of progress concerning his phony case.

"You might think I wasted your time, Mr. Ling, but I don't think that. I am paying you well for your time, so if I'm content to have you chase ghosts, then you will chase ghosts, and not complain about it."

I felt my whole body stiffen. "Tell me why?" I said again, resisting my rising anger. I made sure my tone was not sympathetic or even curious. My goal was to convey my contempt for the way he'd treated me.

Sassoon shook his head. "You don't need to know that. All you need to know is that I expect you to keep investigating my kidnapping and to continue to act as if it had occurred."

I slowly shook my head. "There's nothing to investigate, or am I missing something?"

I ran my hand through my hair and sighed. I could feel sweat pooling in the small of my back.

"You will continue to inquire into the crime I hired you to investigate, Mr. Ling. I expect that of you. Indeed, I demand it from you."

"Why would I do that? I have better things to do than to waste my time chasing an illusory crime. I have a business to run and genuine clients to service." I slowly shook my head. "I don't need your money."

Sassoon smiled a savage smile. I think I knew what was coming. "Furthermore, you will tell no one what I've revealed to you. Understand?"

I nodded.

"If you do not continue, Mr. Ling, I most certainly will destroy you. You will have no life left in Shanghai. I'll see to it that no one — not the triads, not my Jewish community, no one — will give you any business at all, not ever again. You will be finished in Shanghai."

His eyes were cold and flat as he said this.

I believed him.

CHAPTER 43

After I left Sassoon, I telephoned Eli and asked him to meet me at my office. When he arrived, I described my conversation with Sassoon, especially his admission that he had not been kidnapped. Then I said, "Here's the strange part. Sir Victor insists I continue to investigate the crime even though no crime occurred."

Eli looked at me as if I were crazy.

"You heard me right," I said. "Sir Victor made it clear I am to continue to work on the case as if he and I never had this morning's conversation."

Eli looked at me strangely. "What could he have in mind?" he said.

I shook my head. "Nothing I can imagine."

"How are we to proceed then?"

"I haven't worked that out yet. That's why I wanted us to meet. I hope we can come up with a way to move forward, even if we don't know why we're doing so or where we possibly might go with this investigation."

"This is looney," Eli said.

"But perhaps also useful," I said. Eli frowned as if confused. I elaborated.

"Since I have to figure out some way to investigate a crime

that I knew never happened, including knowing when I should stop investigating it because I've taken it as far as I'm able to pretend to take it, you can learn from watching my process, seeing how I approach this bizarre investigation. You'll likely never see a case more peculiar than this one.

"If I'm able to figure this out, and you understand my reasoning, you'll be far along in learning how to approach a simpler, more typical case."

"Okay," Eli said. He shrugged as if he was humoring me. "How do we begin?"

"We'll begin not by looking into an imaginary crime, but by investigating why Sir Victor wants to act as if a crime has been committed."

"Did you ask him?" Eli said.

"He wouldn't tell me," I said, "but he probably wants to deceive someone for reasons we don't yet know. We'll need to figure out who he wants to deceive about the kidnapping, and why.

"If we can learn his motive for this or who he wants to mislead, we might be able to serve him well and solve this non-crime.

CHAPTER 44

LATER THAT SAME DAY I received a coded telephone call from my Dwarf Bandit informant indicating he had important information for me. I called Eli to tell him.

"How can he?" Eli said. "There's no case for him to have information about."

"That's why I want us to go see him. I'm curious to know what he thinks he has that's so important, given what we now know."

Eli and I met at the entrance to the Public Gardens, then walked toward the Garden Bridge to head to Hongkew. We crossed the bridge without incident.

This was a good *joss* day.

We were in sight of Sassoon's luxurious Broadway Mansions, at the confluence of Soochow Creek and the Whangpoo River, heading for the *Seven Swords Inn* on Chapoo Road in Little Tokyo. That was our informant's choice of the place to meet today.

We'd been walking in silence, each, I suppose, thinking about the case and what kind of information our informant could possibly have for us. At least I was thinking about that.

We were within 200 meters of the inn when Eli suddenly yelled, "Look out!"

The phrase had barely escaped his lips as I reflexively spun around to see what he was shouting about.

Eli grabbed my arm and yanked me forward and down toward the sidewalk. As he did this, I felt a sharp pain in my shoulder as a knife sliced through my jacket and shirt, cutting the surface of my skin.

As I hit the ground, the man wielding the knife yelled in *Hu*, "*Ayeeyah! You have been warned. Stop investigating the kidnapping.*" Then he ran off and lost himself in the crowd. I was in shock. I could barely comprehend what he'd said, let alone give chase.

Eli watched the man lose himself in the crowd, then he turned back toward me and helped me up.

We walked over to a bench. I sat. I took off my jacket. Eli tore open the knife slit in my shirt, and we looked at the wound to my shoulder. It seemed superficial. The warning and the implied threat carried by it, however, did not seem superficial.

We decided not to go see my informant. I believed he must have set up the attack against me since he was the only person who knew we were coming to meet him.

We hailed a rickshaw and made our way back across the Garden Bridge to the Shanghai General Hospital on North Soochow Road in the Settlement. I did not want to go to a hospital in Hongkew.

The ride to the hospital, as always with a rickshaw, was bone jarring, but I didn't care. I wanted my wound attended to as quickly as possible so I could turn my focus to the question that now had seized my mind: *Who was it, who so much wanted me to stop looking into a kidnapping that hadn't occurred, that he would harm me if I didn't stop?*

PART THREE

CHAPTER 45

I DID NOT TELL MEI-HUA ABOUT the knife attack. She would have become alarmed. For that reason, because I didn't want to deceive her when she would ask me — as she inevitably would — how my day had been, I did not go to her flat to spend the night. I told her I was tired from my day and that I wanted to go to sleep early. This was true, but obviously omitted essential information.

The next morning, per our arrangement made over the telephone, I went to her flat to have breakfast with her. I brought Bik with me. I told Mei-hua about the assault as we ate breakfast.

"*Ayeeyah!*, Sun-jin, are you all right?"

"Just a nick. I'm fine."

Mei-hua walked over to me and kissed me.

"Maybe just a nick now, but maybe not just a nick another time. You should drop the investigation. Pay attention to the warning before something worse than a small cut happens to you. Sassoon is not worth the risk, not after the way he treated you when you were with the SMP."

I shook my head. "I can't do that. I have to satisfy Sassoon. You understand the stakes here for me, don't you? Sassoon will ruin me if I don't cooperate. I don't have a choice."

"You're in a terrible position," Mei-hua said. "But which is worse, having Sassoon angry with you or being dead?"

I changed the subject, although not to one that had a more obvious answer than the answer to Mei-hua's question.

"What should we do about the fact Tu thinks we're spies? How do we persuade him he's wrong?"

Mei-hua smiled. "I don't know."

It bothered me that Big-Eared Tu thought I was a spy. I probably could convince him he was wrong, based on my history with him, but Mei-hua was a different problem. She was a spy. And, she didn't have a favorable history with Tu. It was a dangerous game she was playing if Tu decided he was correct about her. Perhaps, at great risk to myself, I could persuade him he was wrong about her.

The dangers for Mei-hua with Tu were obvious. Some I could head-off; some I could not.

If Tu became convinced she was spying for the CCP, there was little I could do to protect her from him or from Chiang Kai-shek's KMT- intelligence forces. In the meantime, before Tu might become aware of Mei-hua's espionage activities, I would seek Tu's promise not to act against her. To do this, I would have to spend such good will as I have developed with him over the years.

Tu received me, as always, in his Great Room. It was almost time for the mid-day meal, but I saw no evidence of one being set out for him to consume.

He was impeccably dressed in a long, black silk gown, with gold frog-clasps and gold buttons. He wore the black, small-domed hat favored by elderly men.

After we performed the greeting rituals, we got down to the purpose of my late-morning visit.

"Master Tu, my friend, Wu Mei-hua, told me you believe she is a spy working for the CCP against the KMT."

Tu looked at me with flat eyes. His expression was inscrutable.

"I also believe you're a spy," he said. "But I do not know for whom you work and against whom you spy. Not yet."

These were not the words I wanted hear from this powerful criminal.

"I can assure you we are not spies. We both love our country — love the Republic — and do not work to harm it, either in its war against the Dwarf Bandits or in its struggle to contain, and then later after this war, to defeat Mao."

"Why are you here?" Tu said.

"To ask that you not only not harm Mei-hua, but to beg you to place her under your generous protection. I will vouch for her."

"Why would I do that?"

"You have known me for many years. You know I have never misled you, not even when it might have been to my disadvantage to tell you an unpleasant truth. You have always been able to trust me."

Tu remained silent.

"I am telling you I have no reason to believe Mei-hua is a spy. And because I care for her, I implore you to bestow your greatness upon her, and to protect her from false accusations and deceitful enemies who would mislead you into harming her."

Tu inhaled on his small opium pipe he'd been smoking

when I walked into the Great Room. He blew out the smoke, then shook his head.

"Because of your satisfactory history with me, I will take no steps to harm her unless I learn she is actually engaged as a spy against Chiang. However, I will take no steps to place her under my formal protection. Your woman has not earned that benefit from me. Nor, indeed, have you."

With that cryptic statement, Big-Eared Tu stood up. My meeting with him was over.

I left his home knowing that one of the most powerful criminals in the Celestial kingdom — certainly the most powerful criminal in Shanghai — believed I was a spy and, therefore, that I might be his enemy.

CHAPTER 46

I RETURNED TO MEI-HUA'S FLAT TO report to her about my meeting with Tu. I'd already called Eli. I asked him to meet me there.

I gave them the bad news and warned them both to be careful or to possibly suffer consequences from Tu.

"Tu doesn't know about me, does he?" Eli said.

"Your name never came up," I said. "Just Mei-hua's and mine."

"Nor did it come up when I met with Tu," Mei-hua said.

"Then I should be all right. I will do whatever you decide to do," Eli said, as he looked at Mei-hua.

Afterward, Eli and I rode the electric trolley to my office so we could work on Sassoon's case.

How do you investigate a crime you know never happened?

Determining this would be my first order of business today.

After our recent failed attempt to understand Sassoon's motive when he insisted I investigate a crime he acknowledged had not taken place, Eli and I decided to approach the problem differently than the way I would approach a genuine investigation. We had no other choice if we were, at the very least, to placate Sassoon. The usual methods of investigating a crime would lead us to a dead end.

For the time being, we would ignore Sassoon's possible motive and we would ignore the question how we would know when we have completed our investigation (since we would not be unmasking some criminal, the usual ending to a criminal investigation). For now, we would treat the case as if a crime had occurred, and would try to figure out how we should go about solving it, all this, of course, without having the benefit of any tangible evidence to consider or any witnesses to consult with.

I looked at Eli, and asked the first basic question, one that had been bothering me.

"Since there were no eyewitnesses to the kidnapping — for obvious reasons — or any other evidence of that crime, why did Chief Inspector Chapman believe there had been such a crime?"

Although I asked the question just to give us something to think about and discuss, as a frame of reference, Eli tried to answer it.

"Because Sir Victor's business partners told him so," Eli said. "You said that to me. They believed it because Sir Victor had never before disappeared so silently, without advance, staged fanfare."

"Not quite," I said. "What I told you was that Chapman said to me that Sassoon's partners had come to see him because they were concerned they hadn't heard from him in many weeks. They didn't say he'd been kidnapped. Chapman seems to have arrived at that conclusion on his own.

"So," I said, "I must ask again: Why did the chief inspector and then Sir Victor's partners think he'd been kidnapped? Why didn't they think, for example, that he'd been in an accident somewhere or that he'd become ill?"

When Eli didn't respond, I continued my thought.

"Remember, there was no ransom note or other demand made to the partners that would have alerted them that Sir Victor had been abducted? Besides," I added, "Sir Victor travels for his business all the time."

"Yes, but not without advance publicity." Eli said. "We cannot just ignore that."

I nodded. "Let's set that aside for now."

Eli frowned, and opened his mouth as if he wanted to continue that point. Apparently he thought better of it. He closed his mouth and said nothing.

"I have another question we should explore," I said. "Is there any connection between the killing of Sassoon's comprador and Sir Victor's supposed kidnapping? Didn't the chief inspector say they occurred at the same time and place? Was there anything else that might have connected the two crimes?"

Eli smiled. "Seems like a coincidence that someone — probably Sir Victor — would take advantage of the murder to create the illusion of a second crime. To do so, he'd have had to know in advance about the murder. Are you suggesting Sir Victor was involved in his comprador's—"

"I'm not suggesting anything," I said. "Just following up on random thoughts."

I continued. "Was there anything at the murder scene to suggest to the chief inspector that a second crime — a kidnapping — had taken place outside *Wing On*?"

"Not that I know of," Eli said, "but I only know what you've told me. We've just assumed the murder and kidnapping were connected because that's what you were told by Chapman. Now we know better since we know there was no kidnapping.

"But why would Chapman have believed the crimes were connected or believed there were two crimes?" Eli said. "Is there something he didn't tell you?"

"I don't know," I said. The chief inspector seemed to be open to sharing information with me, but maybe not. Maybe he held something back."

I thought about this, then said, "When I examined the police files, I didn't see anything to suggest to me the crimes were connected. That likely was because the kidnapping was kept secret from most people, including the SMP inspector detectives who were investigating the homicide.

"When I examined the file for the homicide, it was clear to me that all the kidnapping information was deliberately left out of the murder files. Perhaps Chapman just assumed the crimes were connected."

I considered what I wanted to say next, in what direction I wanted to take this discussion. "Let's talk about Sassoon's business partners. What do we know about their role in this?"

"We know they reported Sassoon missing after several weeks when they hadn't heard from him," Eli said. "We also know they never received any demand from the kidnappers."

"I wonder how they responded when Sir Victor suddenly reappeared?" I said.

"There's only one way to find out," Eli said. "We need to meet with them."

I agreed, so I called the three men — Sir Victor's three business partners and investors — who had met with the chief inspector to report Sassoon missing. I set up a separate meeting with each of them.

CHAPTER 47

EARLY THE NEXT MORNING, ELI and I, both nicely dressed in similar dark, double-breasted business suits, black — highly polished — shoes, and black neckties, with our hair carefully groomed — mine with Brilliantine, and his, I suspect, based on its aroma, with Brylcreem, walked into the lobby of the headquarters of the CHINA MERCHANTS' STEAM NAVIGATION COMPANY, a business located at No. 6, the Bund. We rode the lift to the eighteenth floor where the company kept its offices. We had an appointment to meet with Hao Li-feng, one of Sassoon's investors and business partners who had called upon the chief inspector to investigate Sir Victor's mysterious absence from Shanghai.

Hao stood up as we were led into his office. He greeted us warmly, smiled and said, *Zao on — Good morning*, He spoke Mandarin.

After he and I, with Eli standing back one meter, as Confucian custom required, concluded our greeting ritual, I explained that Sir Victor had hired me to find out who had kidnapped him, and why they had done so.

Hao offered us chairs for our meeting. He had green tea served to us. He faced us from behind a large desk.

"Were you and your two colleagues aware that Sir Victor

had been abducted when you went to see the chief inspector?" I said. "Is that why you went to see him?"

"Abducted? *Bú — No.* Not at all. We had no idea. We were concerned that no one among us had seen Victor for many weeks, and not one of us had heard from him during that time. That was highly unusual.

"The inquiries we made through his office gave us no meaningful answers. In fact, the few answers we received from his employees were so evasive that we were worried for his safety, although, at that time, we had no other reason to think we should be.

"We were concerned that Victor might have had an accident and might have developed amnesia or some other such problem, and wandered off. We also were worried that his — meaning, all of ours — businesses and investments would suffer if he did not soon turn up and if the press or other people started asking about him."

Hao removed a cigarette from a small wooden box sitting on his desk and placed the cigarette in the corner of his mouth. He reached across the desk and extended the box, first toward me, and then, when I shook my head no, toward Eli. He also declined the offer. Hao lit his cigarette using a silver Ronson Touch Tip lighter, a type of desktop lighter currently popular among the wealthy, if you can believe what you read in magazine ads.

When Hao again directed his attention to me, I said, "So the chief inspector told you Sir Victor had been kidnapped? That was how you found out?"

Hao slowly shook his head. "No, he did not. He never said that. He did ask us if we received a ransom note or some other demand related to Victor. We hadn't. But we understood the implication of that question, so the chief inspector did not have to say anymore about that.

"When we later discussed this among ourselves, after we left Chapman's office, we concluded Victor had not being kidnapped since there hadn't been any type of demand made. We learned later, after Sir Victor returned, that we'd been wrong, that he had been kidnapped."

"Could Sir Victor have had some business reason to disappear that he didn't tell you about?"

"*Kenong — Maybe.* But that would be unlikely and out of character for him. Victor has always been open with us about his business dealings, even when we weren't directly involved in them. We've all been partners and investors together for many years, and we continually confide in one another.

"Besides, when Sir Victor did return, he told us he's been kidnapped. That should have been the end of that inquiry. We have no reason not to believe him. Why are you implying he hadn't been abducted?"

I decided to test Hao's certainty. "Perhaps Sir Victor has been open with you only with regard to the business matters you know about," I said. "What about matters you don't know about?"

"Are there any?" Hao asked. "How would I know that? If I don't know about them, how can I say?"

"I don't know, but apparently you don't know either," I said.

Hao frowned, but didn't comment. He slowly shook his head as if digesting my vague statement.

"In any event, Mr. Ling, I don't understand your line of inquiry. We all know now that Victor had been kidnapped. We know that because Victor told us so and because you just told me that he has hired you to find out who snatched him."

I tried a different approach. "Did Chief Inspector Chapman say anything to you about the murder of Sir Victor's comprador being related to Sir Victor's kidnapping?"

Hao shook his head. "*Bú — No*. He merely asked if we were aware of the homicide, as we were, of course, from the newspapers. He also asked if we knew of any connection between it and Victor's disappearance. We did not."

"After Sir Victor was released, did he say anything to you that might be helpful to us?"

"Nothing."

"Is there anything we haven't asked you that might be useful for us to know, however trivial it might seem?"

"Not that I know of."

Eli and I stood up, shook hands with Hao, thanked him for seeing us, then left.

That same afternoon, Eli and I kept our appointments with the other two partners who had accompanied Hao to Chapman's office. We learned nothing new from them. Their stories were remarkably consistent with Hao's, and with each other's, almost as if rehearsed.

CHAPTER 48

Pock-Marked Huang waited for Tu to put down his tea bowl, then said, "After having watched the woman for some time now, I believe we have evidence she is a spy for the CCP. She has infiltrated civilian posts in the KMT with several planted Party members. We have identified at least eleven such infiltrations arranged by her. There likely were more we don't yet know about."

"*Ayeeyah!" Tu said.* "It is time to put an end to this."

"*Maskee — No problem.* I will arrange to have the woman eliminated," Huang said.

Tu shook his head. "Not yet. There are many ways to put an end to this that do not require her death. Not right away. Not before she tells us what we should know about her disloyalty and her espionage actions.

"First we must identify everyone she has brought into our fold. We will eliminate them. As soon as we are satisfied no others remain who have not been identified by the woman, then this woman's fate will be the same."

Huang bowed his head.

"Is she working alone?" Tu said.

"We believe she has an accomplice, a man she sometimes meets with, but we are not sure if he's involved or merely is her clandestine, other lover. He is a Communist, the editor of *Slovo*. We are watching him day and night."

Tu snaked his hands and arms up the opposite sleeves of his Mandarin gown. He thought about this.

"No matter," Tu said. "For now, ignore the accomplice, but keep him under watch. When the time is right, after we have eliminated the woman, we will interrogate him to see if he, too, is a spy. Perhaps he will offer us names the woman had not given us.

Tu stood up. "For now, I would like to better evaluate the woman. Bring her to me again. I have questions for her."

CHAPTER 49

AFTER WE COMPLETED OUR INTERVIEWS with Sassoon's business partners, Eli and I returned to my office to consider the implications of having learned nothing new from the three interviews.

"It's not quite that bad, Sun-jin," Eli said. "We did learn one useful thing — at least indirectly."

That statement surprised me.

"*Qivng rang — Excuse me?*" I said. I couldn't imagine what he meant. He and I had been in the same meetings, but he hadn't understood the language we'd conversed in. He had to know less from those meetings than I did because he does not understand Mandarin. At best, all he knew from the three interviews was whatever I had summarized for him after we left each meeting.

"What would that be?" I said.

"What you told me," he said. "That Chief Inspector Chapman did not directly mention to the three men that Sir Victor had been kidnapped."

He was right. "Or, more important," I said, "why Chapman believed that the crime had occurred before he met with these men."

"And," Eli added, "that Chapman hadn't mentioned what it

was about the homicide crime scene that led him to conclude there had been a related crime committed there."

"True," I said. "Those are good observations. What do you think they mean?"

Eli smiled. "I don't know. Do you?"

I shook my head. "Maybe nothing."

"We do know, however," Eli said, "there were no witnesses to the kidnapping because there was no kidnapping. So, going back to our earlier question, what prompted the chief inspector to ask Sir Victor's partners about a ransom note when they visited him? It was as if the chief inspector was suggesting to them that Sir Victor had been kidnapped even though Sir Victor said he hadn't been."

Eli continued. "Maybe the chief inspector was a knowing participant in Sir Victor's faked abduction. Maybe he helped Sir Victor set it up and pull it off, for whatever reason Sir Victor wanted to do that."

"Possibly. I should talk to Chapman about that. We also need to figure out if there is anyone else to interview," I said.

"How about the comprador's family?" Eli said. "It seems to me that the two crimes — the one real and the one made up — must somehow be tied together. We should interview them."

CHAPTER 50

MEI-HUA FINISHED FEEDING BIK HER supper, let her run loose outside, then retrieved her after twenty minutes.

Mei-hua spent the next hour sitting at her kitchen table creating notes she would share with Eli. The notes documented their plan to infiltrate the KMT bureaucracy with CCP members who would report back to the Party concerning the inner workings, and current projects in Shanghai, of Chiang's government.

At 10:30 p.m., Mei-hua climbed into bed and promptly fell asleep. Bik curled up on the bed near her feet.

At about 3:00 a.m., Bik awoke with a start. She lifted her head, turned and looked at Mei-hua, then turned away and faced the bedroom door on the other side of the room. She hopped off the bed.

Bik quietly trotted into the living room and then over to the front door. She stood erect, not moving at all, listening. She sniffed the air several times.

A shadow fell across the lighted opening under the door. Bik ran her snout along the bottom of the door, inhaling the many tell-tale odors available to a dog, but not to a human. Her ears were erect and facing forward; her short tail held high. She bared her teeth in a silent snarl.

Bik abruptly turned away from the door, and briskly, silently, trotted back to the bedroom. She jumped onto the bed and poked her snout firmly into Mei-hua's ribs, over and over again until Mei-hua stirred from her deep sleep.

"Stop it, girl. I'm sleeping. Leave me alone." Mei-hua opened one eye and yawned.

Bik poked her again, harder this time, more insistently, then did this several more times. She licked Mei-hua's cheek. All the while, Bik growled softly.

Mei-hua sat up. "*Ayeeyah!* What's the matter with you, daughter? This isn't like you. Do you want me awake all night? I have things to do tomorrow."

Bik whimpered, jumped off the bed, then ran to the front door.

As Mei-hua came through the bedroom door and entered the living room, her eyes caught movement. She fixed her gaze on the doorknob above Bik. The knob slowly turned.

Mei-hua sprinted to the portion of the wall that would be behind the door when it opened.

She waited, mentally and physically placing herself into *Shaolin* attack mode as she anticipated the entry of an intruder. She breathed deeply and slowly.

The door opened.

Light from the hallway stole into the apartment. Bik growled, but no longer softly.

Mei-hua crouched behind the opened door, pouring the weight of her left leg into her right leg. She slowed her breathing so her chest barely moved. Her eyes narrowed. She waited.

The intruder stepped into the living room and then quietly closed the door behind him. He stiffened when he saw Mei-hua crouched behind it. The man reflexively stepped back.

Mei-hua immediately pushed off her full right leg, spun once, and thrust her left leg forward and upward. Done correctly, this kick would be a debilitating *Shaolin* offensive move.

The kick had not been done correctly.

Mei-hua's foot barely caught the intruder under his chin, the intended target, on the right side of his neck. He staggered backward, then fell to the floor, but quickly rebounded. He stood again before Mei-hua could follow-up her first strike.

The intruder pulled a knife from his belt, and took a step forward.

As the man moved toward Mei-hua, Bik ran over to the intruder and bit his left leg, sinking her teeth in just above the ankle. She held on as the man shook his leg and spun around once to launch Bik away.

Bike held on.

The man raised his knife to stab Bik, cursing as he bent over to reach her.

As the intruder raised his arm to stab Bik, Mei-hua kicked him in the side of his head, knocking him against the wall. The knife flew from his hand.

Mei-hua closed in to finish her attack.

The man struck Mei-hua with his fist, just above her lip, breaking her nose. She fell backward to the floor.

A torrent of blood gushed over Mei-hua's night dress. Blood spurted into the air, temporarily blinding her.

Bik again bit the man's leg.

The last thing Mei-hua was aware of, her head spinning before she blacked out, was the sound of someone running down the stairs, and the sound of the building's front door slamming. She was alone with Bik, who licked her cheek as Mei-hua swooned. Everything went dark.

CHAPTER 51

I SAT IN THE CHIEF INSPECTOR'S office, across the desk from him. As usual, I had to wait while he filled and lit his pipe.

"Good to see you again," he finally said to me. I doubted he meant it. "What can I do for you?"

"I have a few more questions you might be able to clear up for me in connection with the investigation I'm conducting for Sir Victor."

Chapman frowned. "When I shut down your investigation for the SMP, I told you he hadn't been kidnapped, that it had been a misunderstanding. You're wasting everyone's time pursuing this, including Sir Victor's time."

"And yet, Chief Inspector, to this day Sir Victor insists he'd been kidnapped. I would think he should know, if anyone would. That's good enough for me."

This statement, which probably reminded him of a similar statement he made to me when he asked me to handle the kidnapping investigation, clearly bothered the chief inspector. It was as if I was choosing between his word and Sassoon's. The odd thing is that as long as I have known Chapman, going back more than fifteen years, he has always deferred to Sassoon. *Why not now?*

"Please indulge me, Chief Inspector. I don't want to be

caught between you and Sir Victor. I've suffered from that situation in the past, as you know."

Chapman stared at me for a few seconds. He puffed once on his pipe, which appeared to have gone cold. He relit it, then said, "What do you want to know?"

"When you first told me Sir Victor had been kidnapped, what made you think that?"

"His business partners came to see me because they hadn't seen him or heard from him for more than four or five weeks."

"Did they say he'd been kidnapped?"

"No. They didn't know what had happened to him, but they were concerned to avoid rumors that might affect his and their business holdings."

This was not what Sassoon's business partners told me.

"Did something in particular about his absence suggest to you he'd been kidnapped?"

"No."

"Why, then, did you ask Sir Victor's partners if they had received a ransom note or some other demand?"

The chief inspector's face reddened. His lifted his chin. "I didn't ask them that. Did they say I did?"

"Yes."

"Then you misunderstood me. I'd told you there wasn't a ransom note or other demand. I didn't say I asked Sir Victor's partners that question. I never did. You just assumed I had."

I let this pass, although I wondered whether it was Chapman or Sir Victor's partners who were lying about this. I also wondered why anyone would do so.

"Was there something about the comprador's homicide that suggested to you Sir Victor had been kidnapped, that he had even been at *Wing On* with his comprador that morning?"

"No. The killing was just a routine murder, although, I suppose, the killing of a comprador is not ever routine."

"Then why did you tell me that Sir Victor had been with his comprador that morning and that he'd been abducted as part of the murder?"

"Because that's what the evidence first pointed to when we investigated the homicide," Chapman said.

"What evidence? I didn't come across that when I reviewed the Murder Book or the other homicide files."

"Of course you didn't, Old Boy. That evidence is confidential, a police matter, somethings I couldn't show or tell you about. You don't have the official status necessary to know about that. Be satisfied you got to see the Murder Book and most of the official files."

This was becoming irritating. It seemed the chief inspector was intentionally avoiding answering my questions. I tapped my foot to calm down.

"Sir, with all due respect, that doesn't make sense. You said at the time you hired me that you believed Sir Victor had been kidnapped when his comprador was murdered. Now you say Sir Victor had not been kidnapped. What evidence is there that will resolve this?

"If you're concerned about wasting Sir Victor's time, you should make that evidence available to me so we can clear this up."

The chief inspector stood up. "I have work to do now. Thank you for coming by."

He walked me to his office door.

CHAPTER 52

As I left Chapman's office, I stopped at his secretary's desk and used her telephone to call Eli. I arranged for him to meet me downstairs in front of the SMP central headquarters.

I said, "Let's go to the comprador's home and talk to his family."

We rode an electric trolley to Frenchtown. We had to watch four streetcars pass us by before one stopped for us. The first four had Kwantung troops aboard.

We did not call ahead to arrange an appointment with the comprador's family, although proper decorum required that we do so. I knew that an advance call from me for an appointment would have been politely, but firmly, rebuffed, and no appointment made, since I had no prior relationship with the family. We Chinese are very private about our family matters.

But if we just showed up at the family's front door, as we planned to do, we would be admitted to the house, although begrudgingly. No self-respecting Confucian or Taoist would turn us away, and acknowledge our bad manners by doing so, causing us to lose face.

Sir Victor's dead comprador, named Xun Gan-li, had functioned as the exclusive intermediary between Sassoon's various businesses and Shanghai's Chinese business community.

Xun Gan-li not only successfully conducted business on behalf of Sassoon, especially in connection with the management and operation of Sassoon's real estate properties, but, using much flattery and deceit, he had left his taipan with the naïve impression that he, Sir Victor, had been the brains behind their joint success.

We arrived at Xun Gan-li's brick house, located on Avenue Edouard VII, at 10:00 a.m. We wanted to catch the important family members at home before they began their various daily duties, some of which would be performed outside the house. Xun Gan-li had lived in the house with three wives and eleven children.

We knocked on the door. It was opened by a coolie-servant woman.

"*Zao an,* Auntie — *Good morning,* Auntie," I said.

She looked at us with narrowed, suspicious eyes. Before I could say more, she started to close the door. I blocked it with my foot, and pushed it open again.

"*Wō jiao Ling Sun-jin — My name is Ling Sun-jin.* We are here to see Xun Gan-li's eldest son. I don't know his name. We have business concerning his father. I am a private investigator."

The woman looked into my eyes, gave me White Eyes to register her distain for me, then quickly closed the door. I had no idea if she would now ignore us, leaving us standing outside, or if she would convey our message to the eldest son.

After five or so minutes, she re-opened the door. This time, again without saying a word, but also this time without giving us White Eyes. She beckoned us, with a curt wave of her hand as she turned away, to follow her.

Xun Gan-li's eldest son, Xun Min, stood and greeted us as we entered a room he'd been seated in.

"*Zao an*," he said. "Welcome to my home. I don't believe we've ever met. Do you prefer we speak Mandarin or English?" he asked, speaking Mandarin.

"English, please," I said for Eli's benefit.

Xun spoke with a cultivated British accent. He'd obviously been educated in Britain. He spoke the flawless, foreign Oxbridge English of the educated university class.

"Thank you for receiving us in your home without an appointment," I said. I introduced myself as a PI, introduced Eli as my colleague, and said we were investigating the murder of his father. In accordance with my instructions, however, first from Chapman, then from Sassoon, I did not mention Sir Victor or the kidnapping.

"What is your interest in my father's murder?" Xun asked.

"The SMP has asked me to take a fresh look at the crime. I am assisting them." He had no need to know the truth about the identity of my client.

He nodded. "I doubt there is anything I can tell you about it. I wasn't there. I only know what the two SMP inspector detectives, who investigated the crime, told me, and what I read in the *North-China Daily News.*

"Did your father go to *Wing On* alone?" I said.

"I don't know, but I suppose so. No one else was seen there with him as far as I know."

"Do you know why he went there that morning?"

"No, not for sure. He had mentioned to me while we ate breakfast that morning that he had business with the president of *Wing On*, something on behalf of my father's taipan, who at the time was away from Shanghai visiting a foreign country."

That last was news to me. "Could your father have been there alone to do his own shopping?"

Xun shook his head. "No. My father never shopped. He despised shopping. He always used one of our servants to shop for him."

I thought about where I wanted to go with this.

"With your father's death, will you now become comprador for Sir Victor Sassoon as tradition dictates?" I was looking for motive.

Xun's face darkened. "I should, but I will be denied that traditional honor." He shook his head as if he'd just had an evil thought.

"Although I worked many years with my father as a junior comprador, training for the day when I would follow him into that position after he retired or died, as custom and practice dictate, I will not be permitted to step into his shoes."

"How do you know?" I said.

"My father once told me that Sir Victor had said to him that he did not feel I was qualified to ever be a comprador, that I was too lazy. Apparently he has not changed his mind.

"Immediately after Sir Victor returned to Shanghai, I met with him to ask if I could begin the process of shifting my father's responsibilities to me. He refused me that traditional honor. Sir Victor said I am not the person he wished to put into his operation in my father's place."

So much for motive.

"I'm sorry that's the case," I said. "You must be disappointed."

There's a lot of money at stake there, I thought.

"Perhaps Sir Victor felt his operation requires someone with more experience with real estate," I said, hoping to mollify him.

His face and neck turned crimson. "You'll have to ask him. I don't know why he's denying me my rightful place as my father's successor. I have never in my life been lazy. I don't know why Sir Victor would think such a thing."

With that, Xun stood up and bowed his head slightly. This was his signal it was time for us to leave.

I said, "Are there other family members or servants we may talk to?"

Xun shook his head. "Our meeting is over. You must leave now. Don't return. You are not welcome here."

CHAPTER 53

POCK-MARKED HUANG'S MEN BROUGHT MEI-HUA to Big-Eared Tu.

She stood in front of Tu in his Great Room. She bowed her head slightly as Confucian custom required a younger person to do when first in the presence of an adult male authority figure.

Mei-hua breathed heavily and looked at the floor to avoid frowning at Tu. This contrite act she performed with her head disgusted her. This, and other submissive Confucian customs, had been one of the many things Mei-hua rejected when she joined the CCP.

"You have been lying to me, Miss Wu," Tu said. He spoke softly, almost inaudibly. His gentle tone was laced with menace.

Mei-hua lifted her head and looked in Tu's eyes. "With all due respect, Master Tu, I have not lied to you. I know how foolish such behavior would be. I am not a fool."

"My information says otherwise."

"Why was I forced to come here?" Mai-hua said.

"I am offering you an opportunity to end your life in a merciful manner," Tu said. "I know you are a spy for the CCP. There is no doubt about that.

"Tell me who your accomplices are, the names of the people

you've embedded into the KMT, and the positions you've placed them in. Then, if you have been truthful, I will see to it that your end will be swift and painless. Otherwise, well, you understand the rules of war."

"I am not a spy. You are guessing, Master Tu. You have no proof because there is no proof. You merely are acting out because you failed in your attempt to assassinate me last night.

"Now, for some reason, you believe you need an excuse to eliminate me, although I don't know why you would want to do so or why you might feel the need for an excuse to do so if that's what you've decided."

Tu frowned. He cocked his head to one side. *Had Huang acted against my orders and attempted to kill this woman?*

"Attempt to assassinate you?" he said. "I did no such thing. What are you talking about?"

Mei-hua briefly described the attempt on her life the previous night.

"Are you saying you know nothing about that?" She shook her head and frowned to indicate she was skeptical. She stared hard at Tu, no longer intimidated by him.

"I wondered about the strange state of your face," Tu said, "but did not want to be impolite by asking you." He bowed his head, then said, "Miss Wu, if I wanted you dead, you would be dead. As I indicated, I know nothing about the attempt on your life. You have my word."

"Your reputation, Master Tu, is that you know everything of consequence that happens in Shanghai," Mei-hua said.

"That's correct. I do know everything of consequence in our city. But perhaps an attempt on your life is not of much consequence, Miss Wu, except to you."

Mei-hua stood up. "I am leaving, Master Tu. I would appreciate it if you will keep out of my life."

"As a gesture of good will because you mistakenly believe I tried to kill you, I will permit you to live. For now. But be careful what you do with this gift. We will be watching you," Tu said. "Be mindful who you associate with and be careful of the things you do."

CHAPTER 54

MEI-HUA AND BIK CAME OVER to my flat early this evening. I was stunned when I saw her.

"What happened to you?" I asked, as I took her into my arms and hugged her. I then leaned my head back away from her face to see her better. Mei-hua's nose was bandaged. The area around her eyes was purple, yellow, and black.

"Our daughter is a hero," Mei-hua said.

She explained her misadventure the past evening and also told me about her meeting with Tu. She said she believed that Tu knew nothing about the attempt on her life, except what she'd told him.

We sat at my kitchen table after I'd boiled water for tea. Bik was curled up underneath, her snout resting on my foot.

"Why would someone break into my flat?" Mei-hua said. "No one could think I have anything worth stealing, because I don't. And why didn't he kill me when I passed out?"

I thought about how I wanted to answer.

"I don't think this was a burglary attempt or an attempt to assassinate you. It probably was meant as a message for me, a message that I should quit my investigation for Sir Victor because, by continuing it, I am placing you in danger."

"Who would do that?" Mei-hua said. She seemed more curious than concerned.

I thought briefly about that. "It could be Tu, in spite of what you think. He's a shrewd manipulator, although I don't know why he would care about Sassoon's kidnapping. Or, it could be Inspector Detective Harue. He seems to resent every case I engage in.

"Maybe it was the person who murdered Sassoon's comprador, since the murder and the fake kidnapping might be connected," I said.

I raised my eyebrows and shrugged to indicate I actually had no idea, that my answer was pure speculation.

"Why would a message be sent to you, using me as bait?" Mei-hua said. "Why not just threaten you directly?"

"To get my attention. Threatening to harm me or to kill me would be a wasted effort. I wouldn't consider dropping a case because I was threatened. Threats come with being a PI.

"But threatening you, that's different," I said. "Whoever made the threat, if that's the message, knows I would pay attention to that."

"But why?" Mai-hua said. "You said the kidnapping wasn't real. There was no crime. Who would care if you investigate it?"

"Maybe the comprador's murderers. Perhaps they don't know the kidnapping was fake, so they worry that my investigation of that crime might lead me to also solve their crime," I said.

CHAPTER 55

THE NEXT MORNING, I WAS in my office sitting at my desk trying to decide how I should deal with Mei-hua's problem with Tu. I also wondered who would have tried to threaten her as a warning to me. I doubted it was Tu. He would have directly ordered me to stop my investigation, and I would have listened to him. Tu did not need to utter threats, indirect or otherwise.

Suddenly, my office door flew open. It banged against the wall. Two Kwantung soldiers rushed in and stopped on either side of my desk, facing me. They pointed their rifles and bayonets at me.

JMP Inspector Detective Harue strutted into my office, his hands clasped behind his back. He stopped in front of my desk.

"*Hai!* You defied my order?" he said, his voice rising in pitch as he said this. I noticed his right hand now moved to the handle of the sword he wore.

"How dare you break into my office like this," I said. "I'll report you to the SMP. You don't have jurisdiction here."

"I ordered you to stay out of the occupied districts, yet you entered Chapei at least two times I'm aware of to meet with someone."

"Why are you doing this?" I said. I spoke softly, hoping not to fuel his anger.

"Yes, I went to Chapei," I said. "I had to. I need to earn a living. My work took me there. I had people to meet with. Informants. That's what a PI does." I sighed. "I also live there. I entered Chapei to go to my home."

The soldiers moved closer to me.

"I haven't interfered with the Kwantung. I'm just trying to do my work. I've always shown respect to you and to the Imperial army."

"Why am I doing this, you ask?" Harue smiled.

"I don't need a reason to bar you from the occupied districts," he said. "Even if I had a reason, I would not tell you. It is enough that I ordered you to stay out of the districts, yet you chose to defy me. Now you will see who has power and who does not."

With that statement, he nodded at one of the soldiers who moved around the desk and pressed the tip of his bayonet against the base of my neck.

"Stand up," Harue said. "Put your hands behind your back."

I did as I was told. I began to shake. I couldn't stop myself.

The second soldier moved behind me and bound my wrists together with coarse rope.

Harue laughed. "Since you seem to have an unusual desire to be in Chapei in spite of my order to you, I will grant your wish. I am moving you to a civilian internment camp in Chapei. You will live there for the duration of our war."

CHAPTER 56

I WAS PUSHED, OCCASIONALLY PRODDED WITH the tip of a bayonet, and at times grabbed by my arm as I was dragged outside to the back of an army transport truck. One of the soldiers untied my wrists, then motioned for me to climb up the portable steps into the truck's troop-carrying area.

I sat on a long wooden bench. Two armed Kwantung soldiers sat across from me, their rifles out of my reach, but pointed in my general direction. We were the only ones in the troop-transport area of the truck.

When we arrived at the internment camp, I was nudged out of the truck by the point of a bayonet on a rifle held by one of the guards who had accompanied me from my office.

I looked around as I climbed down the four steps from the truck.

The internment camp was large. It seemed to consist of a single, three-story wooden building located on the site of the former high school known as the *Courtyard of the Happy Way*. I had heard of this camp. It was known by the same name as the high school. It was located at the intersection of North Longhuan and Baise Roads. Harue had sent me back to Chapei as he said he would.

The *Courtyard of the Happy Way* had been a well-known

school in Shanghai before the war. It sat on twenty-three acres. It now was surrounded by a 10-meter high fence(I later learned it was electrified) topped with barbed wire. There were elevated watch towers spaced at regular intervals along the fence. These, as far as I could tell by looking up at them, were manned by guards having rifles or machine guns. Other guards, accompanied by dogs on leashes, patrolled the perimeter of the camp, walking just outside the fence.

I was taken to an administration office (the former school administrator's office, according to the sign over the door) to be processed. I was given a red armband and told to wear it at all times. It identified me as Chinese. Other nationalities, I soon would learn, wore other color armbands to identify them.

I was assigned to Room 216, on the second floor. This was a former classroom now filled with thin mattresses scattered across the floor. I learned later that the room held 83 internees. Other classrooms, I would learn, were as crammed.

I entered Room 216, followed by a guard, with instructions to place my bedroll on the floor, and then report to the doctor's office for my physical examination.

When we entered Room 216, I saw an elderly man sweeping the floor with a long-handle straw broom. He looked up and nodded at me as the guard and I walked in. I found an empty space near a wall. I dropped my bedroll there. Then I walked over to the man.

"*Ayeeyah, Uncle,*" I said. "*Heya — Hello.*"

I noticed his eyes look at my armband, confirming I was an internee, then shift to glance at the guard who watched us from across the room.

"*Heya*" he said in return. He resumed his sweeping.

I didn't know if he spoke Mandarin (I was sure the guard did not) so I spoke to him in *Hu.*

"I must go with the guard now to continue my processing," I said. "May we speak later, Uncle? I hope you will teach me much about living here. I am new at this."

The old man bowed his head slightly and resumed sweeping. He said nothing.

Three hours later the old man and I sat on the steps in front of the brick school building. His name was Wang Hsin. He said he was 62 years old. He looked much older.

"I have been at the *Courtyard of the Happy Way* for almost seven months," he said. "I was editor of the English-language newspaper, *Shanghai News.* Apparently, the Dwarf Bandits did not like our stories about the Kwantung and their imperial war against our country.

"I am told that this camp was set up to hold Shanghainese who the Dwarf Bandits fear might cause them trouble because of our knowledge of military, economic, religious, communications, or other such matters. There are many teachers, religious leaders, and politicians here. What was your offense?"

"None," I said, "as far as I'm concerned. I have had a long-running feud with a JMP inspector detective who also holds some rank with the Kwantung. He decided it was time to exercise his authority over me and time to restrict my ability to earn a living as a private investigator. I disobeyed his order to stay out of Chapei, so here I am, back in Chapei."

I waited for him to comment, but he said nothing. I continued. "Tell me about this camp, Uncle."

He retrieved a partly smoked cigarette from his pants pocket. He put the unlit cigarette into the corner of his mouth.

"*Ayeeyah*. Life here is hard. You will see that soon enough," he said. "We wake up every day to hunger, to guard dogs threatening us, to guards beating us. We suffer much illness.

"The camp's several interned doctors, most of whom are Celestials, are not permitted to treat the ill, although we need them to do so.

"Overall, we are very crowded. There is no privacy. Not even between men and women. There is no escape at night from the sounds of fornication. It is embarrassing for the children. You will see that tonight when Room 216 fills up."

My stomach roiled from anxiety.

"Sanitation is almost non-existent. We have bed-bugs, flies, lice, and other vermin. There are only two toilets for every eight hundred people. The toilets rarely flush. The lines for the bathrooms are unending, as you will learn. There is no toilet paper. We improvise for now with leaves and old newspapers.

"We have limited water to drink, limited food to eat. The water is contaminated, the food usually spoiled. We suffer from malnutrition and, typically, from malaria, typhoid, and whooping cough. You soon will see this, too."

Just then a guard came along and strode over to us, his bayonet pointed toward us. He stopped about three meters away.

"*Hai!* Move along, old man," he said, directing his bayonet toward Wang's chest. He then turned his attention to me.

"Walk with me. It is time for you to be photographed and finger-printed. Don't try anything. I will be right behind you."

CHAPTER 57

NINE DAYS HAD PASSED SINCE Sun-jin's incarceration.

Sassoon was furious. Even though he'd frequently shunned meetings with Sun-jin, now he interpreted Sun-jin's absence as an affront to his authority.

He hadn't heard from Sun-jin in ten days. All his efforts to locate him had failed. He assumed Sun-jin either had left the city without obtaining his permission or that he'd died. Neither condition was acceptable to him.

Sir Victor dispatched all his resources to locate Sun-jin. On the third day, his new comprador — Luk Xu — met with him to report that Sun-jin had been located.

"*Shi* — *Yes,* Master Victor. We have had good *joss.* Ling Sun-jin is alive. We know where he is." He described Sun-jin's circumstances.

Sassoon immediately contacted Chief Inspector Chapman who, in turn, contacted his counterpart at the JMP. In addition, Sassoon offered more than enough *squeeze* for the JMP police and for Kwantung officers at the internment camp to have Sun-jin released.

Within ten hours, Sun-jin walked warily out of the *Courtyard of the Happy Way*, and, although unshaven and unbathed, and much thinner than he'd been the last time he and Sassoon met, was met by Sir Victor's body guard who brought him directly to Sassoon House.

CHAPTER 58

I STOOD ACROSS THE DESK FROM Sir Victor. I was embarrassed to be there in my unkempt, malodorous condition. I knew how foul-smelling I was, and could only imagine how I might appear with my scraggly beard, unwashed hair, some facial scabs, and my filthy, wrinkled clothing.

Sir Victor was unusually gracious.

"Sit, please, Sun-jin.". He smiled. "You look like hell. May I get you some tea?"

"No thank you, Sir Victor." I lowered myself into a chair. It was more difficult than I expected. I was weak and fatigued. "I'm not sure I could hold down tea or any other drink right now."

"I'll keep this short, Sun-jin. When we are done here, I will have my First Boy take you to your home so you can bathe and rest. I will send my physician over today to see you, at my cost, of course."

I said nothing.

The thought of returning home raised concerns for me. It caused me to think of Mei-hua. *She had no idea what had become of me during the past nine days.*

Would she be angry when I suddenly reappeared out of nowhere, with no word from me for more than a week?

Sassoon said, "I want you to wrap up your investigation in the next week, at the latest. Let me know your results, then send me your final bill."

So much for time to recuperate.

Is he crazy? What am I to report to him? Should I say: The result of my investigation is that I did not find the criminal who had not committed the crime that had never occurred?

CHAPTER 59

MEI-HUA WAS NOT ANGRY WITH me. She had been worried and, therefore, angry during the time I was missing and silent. Her attitude changed as soon as she saw me and, as ragged and foul-smelling as I was, as soon as we'd held each other.

The next morning, I rang up Eli and asked him to meet me the next day at the office so we could review the state of our case. I would bring him up to date on Sassoon's instructions to me. I was curious to see his reaction. I suspected he would first laugh, then shake his head in wonder.

When Eli picked up his telephone, and I'd identified myself, he said, "I've tried to reach you. Where've you been?"

"*Ayeeyah!* It's a long story. I'll tell you tomorrow morning."

Eli and I spread the case files out over a large table I'd bought from the public library's surplus room for this purpose. Then, before we started reviewing the files, I described what had happened to me.

When we finished discussing this, I said, "Sassoon still

insists we solve the crime that hadn't occurred. He wants us to conclude it promptly."

"Are you able to in your condition?" Eli said.

I shrugged. "Do I have a choice?"

"I don't understand," Eli said. "What does he actually expect from us?"

I shrugged. "I don't know, and, as usual, he wasn't forthcoming about that."

I paused to think how I wanted to state my next thought so I wouldn't unduly alarm Eli.

"I don't hold out much hope we'll resolve this. I expect that I — and perhaps you, too — will be in for a difficult time from now on from Sir Victor."

"I don't know that we can do anything to change that, can we?" Eli said.

"At this point, I don't particularly care about me, but I am concerned about how this might affect you," I said.

Eli and I reviewed all the files. When we finished, I said, "Let's list the unanswered questions we still must resolve, and see if we can apply the information we do know to resolve them.

"Here is what I see as questions we still need to answer." I stood up and began to pace around the table, thinking out loud.

Why was Sir Victor's comprador murdered?

Who had a motive to kill him?

Was Sir Victor supposed to be with the comprador at *Wing On*?

Was an attempt made to kidnap Sir Victor at *Wing On*?

Did Chief Inspector Chapman at first believe Sir Victor had been kidnapped?

If yes, if he did believe that, what caused him to change his mind and call off the investigation before Sir Victor returned?

Where was Sir Victor during the four or five weeks the chief inspector believed he'd been kidnapped?

Why has Sir Victor kept his actual whereabouts secret during that period?

"That's all I can think of at the moment," I said. "Can you think of anything I've missed?"

"Maybe," Eli said. "I think that's everything except the obvious, overall question: Why does Sassoon think it's in his interest to have us solve a crime that we all know didn't occur?

CHAPTER 60

AFTER WE COMPLETED LISTING THE open-questions list, Eli and I reviewed the case files, page by page. We went back to the very beginning, and tried to envision the purported kidnapping as the chief inspector had first described it to me.

I walked to the old ice box I kept in my office and took out two bottles of *Clover* beer. I gave one to Eli.

I sat down at my desk and thought about the investigation and about the questions Eli and I had listed.

Then it hit me.

I recalled what the murdered comprador's son had said when Eli and I interviewed him.

Xun Min had said that his father had mentioned in passing at breakfast that Sassoon had been in a foreign country the morning the comprador had been murdered?

I thought about that.

Why hadn't Sassoon ever mentioned his trip to me?

Why had he kept that trip secret? Which foreign country had Sassoon gone to?

Who would benefit if this trip was known? Who could that knowledge harm if it were known?

I clearly had to meet again with Sir Victor and get answers

to these questions. It seemed to me that this secret might be the key to the comprador's murder and to Sir Victor's persistence concerning the fake kidnapping.

PART FOUR

CHAPTER 61

I ARRANGED TO MEET WITH SIR Victor.

At first, we engaged in our usual greeting and sparring match. Sassoon said I was wasting time by coming to see him if all I intended to do was to summarize the poor state of my investigation. I said I was not there to report to him, that I had a question or two, and that I was close to understanding who murdered the comprador and why they'd done so. I also said I was close to understanding why he insisted I investigate the fake kidnapping.

He sat up straighter and nodded. Apparently, my last statement peaked his curiosity.

"Go on," he said. "Ask your questions, then tell me why you think I have you working on my investigation."

"You told me you were away from Shanghai when your comprador was shot. Where were you?"

Sassoon hesitated and frowned. "Do you need to know that?"

"*Ayeeyah!* Of course I do. That's why I asked."

"If I tell you, do you agree to keep the reason confidential?"

I raised my eyebrows as if to say, *I would give you White Eyes for that question except you wouldn't understand my meaning.*

"I agree," I said. "Everything we talk about or I learn in the course of my investigation is confidential."

Sir Victor took a deep breath, the first time ever he's shown any hesitancy about anything in my presence.

"I was in Japan for most of the time. Some of that time, of course, I spent traveling there and traveling back to Shanghai."

That surprised me, considering China and Japan have been at war since the summer of 1937.

"Are you a spy for the Kwantung?" I said.

Sir Victor frowned and shook his head as if to wonder how I could ask such a stupid question.

"Don't be foolish. If I were, do you think I would have told you I was in Japan?"

"Why then?"

Sir Victor put a match to the end of a cigar, and stared at it as if doing so would help him find the words to explain his trip to me.

"As you might know, the Japanese and Jewish communities have a strong bond that grew out of events that occurred in 1904, at the beginning of the Russo-Japanese War. We also have a strong cultural bond."

This was news to me. "What was the Jewish-Japanese bond concerning the 1904 war?"

"When Russia and Japan were flexing their imperial muscles in Manchuria and Korea, heading toward a war with each other, as we now know, Japan was not in a position to finance a large-scale conflict. It seemed inevitable Japan would lose a protracted war unless she could secure financing. She set out to find a large loan with favorable terms to underwrite the conflict's costs.

"Not one country agreed to make a loan to Japan, although

she was in dire straits and stood to lose much of her empire to Russia.

"Either Japan would find the money to fight a war or she would have to precipitously withdraw from Korea and Manchuria, ceding those countries to Russia.

"Russia, aware of Japan's situation, stepped up its aggression in Manchuria and Korea as Japan helplessly watched.

"Then, late in 1904, as Japan and Russia closed in on war or on Japan's withdrawal from Manchuria and Korea, Jacob Schiff, chairman of Kuhn, Loeb & Co., a Wall Street investment bank in New York City, put together a consortium of small, Jewish-run banks in New York that raised $200 million in bonds for Japan. Schiff, on behalf of this group, then made a very favorable loan to the Emperor.

The rest, as you know, is history. The underdog, Japan, went on to defeat Russia in the Russo-Japanese War in 1904-1905. Ever since, the government of Japan has had a warm place in its heart for the Jewish culture and population."

"Interesting story," I said, "but what does that have to do with your trip to Japan?"

"That special relationship provided me with the basis for my trip. I went to Japan to seek financial aid from the Imperial government to help Jewish refugees who are living in Shanghai. I also hoped to obtain financial aid so I, together with some local charitable organizations, can bring more Jewish refugees here before the Nazis slam the door shut on Jewish emigration."

Sassoon took a long pull on his cigar.

"Japan came through for me," he said, "although the trip took longer than I anticipated."

Sir Victor hesitated as if he was considering something else he wanted to tell me.

"As further evidence of the close relationship between Japan and the Jewish people, the Emperor's representatives pointed out to me that the Nazis, since 1939, have been pressuring Japan to round up Shanghai's Jews and ship them to Germany for relocation to concentration camps scattered throughout Europe. Japan has refused to comply."

Sassoon's explanation did not answer all my questions. "Interesting," I said, "but why keep your trip secret? Many people in Shanghai know of your efforts to support Jewish immigrants."

"I kept my trip secret to keep members of the Municipal Council from discovering its purpose.

"You must know from various newspaper accounts that the Council has been considering limiting, or even stopping, Jewish immigration into the city. If Council members had learned of the purpose of my trip, they undoubtedly would have passed such restrictive legislation as quickly as possible, probably before I even returned from Japan."

I nodded. "I see."

"And, of course, to add to that problem, there also is the problem that several Council members despise me because I'm Jewish and because I hold the mortgage secured by their precious Shanghai Club. In these precarious financial times, that gives me great power over a club that twice refused to allow me to become a member.

Sassoon stared at me for a few seconds. Then he continued, "You said you are close to solving my comprador's murder, revealing the kidnapping plot against me, and disclosing why I insisted on having you investigate a crime that never occurred. Tell me."

I shook my head. "No, sir, not yet. I want to think through a few questions I still have, then I'll disclose everything to you, to my girlfriend — Wu Mei-hua — and to my PI colleague, Eli Ben-David Reuben. I'll do it all at the same time.

CHAPTER 62

IN SPITE OF WHAT I said to Sassoon, I really had only one question I still wanted to think about: How had Sassoon's trip to Japan and the fact he'd kept it secret, related, if at all, to the murder of the comprador? What tied them together?

I was pretty sure I knew the answer, but I wanted to wait a day or two, turning this over in my head, before calling everyone together.

I left Sir Victor and headed back to my office to talk with Eli. We had arranged to meet there after my meeting with Sassoon. I wanted to alert him to the fact that we were winding down now, and that I soon would have answers to our questions. I also wanted to again look over some of the case files to prepare for another meeting I'd set up for later today.

Eli seemed nervous when I told him we were coming to the end of our investigation.

"Does that mean I'll be finished here, that you won't continue to teach me how to be a PI?"

"Not at all. It just means that we will work together on other matters, some interesting, some not, but all worked on by us together to generate income."

I could see him relax as his posture softened.

CHAPTER 63

After Sun-jin and he met at Sun-jin's office, after Sun-jin had left for his other meeting, Eli remained to review files for three cases unrelated to Sassoon or to the comprador's murder that Sun-jin and he would begin investigating the next day.

The telephone rang. It was Mei-hua. She wanted to speak with Eli.

"We should talk," she said. "We should talk alone. And soon."

"Sun-jin's not here," Eli said. "He's meeting with the chief inspector. I don't expect him to return for an hour or more. We can meet here."

Mei-hua arrived ten minutes later.

"I have been thinking about the danger you and I have placed ourselves in concerning the CCP," Mei-hua said. "Danger from Inspector Detective Harue, from the Kwangtung, and from Big-Eared Tu, all who think we are spies for the CCP."

"We are spies," Eli said, "in a manner of speaking."

"Of course we are, and we're playing a dangerous game that we can only lose in this time of war," Mei-hua said. "I propose we end that activity for now, then resume it after China has defeated the Dwarf Bandits."

Eli frowned, then shrugged. "I suppose you're right. One of those three is likely to strike out against us if we keep up our activities. Or, if they even think we are keeping up our activities, even if we're not doing so.

"I agree," Mei-hua said. "We'll go dormant, but we must do it in a way that will let those three know we are not engaging in espionage," he said. "Otherwise it could be a futile step and not protect us."

CHAPTER 64

THE NEXT MORNING, ELI, MEI-HUA, and I assembled in Sir Victor's office. I introduced Mei-hua and Eli to him, and Sassoon to them.

When we all were seated, I said, "*Ayeeyah!* I have figured out why Sir Victor's comprador was murdered and why there was a plot to kidnap Sir Victor. I'll likely repeat some things some of you already know, but others don't, so please accept that inconvenience as part of my explanation."

I looked at everyone, my eyes lingering on Sir Victor's eyes longer than on the others, until everyone, including Sassoon, either nodded their assent or had expressed it verbally.

I faced Sassoon. "I also have figured out why you had me chasing a crime that we know never occurred."

Sir Victor said nothing. He shrugged one shoulder and looked hard into my eyes, squinting slightly.

"It all began with you, Sir Victor, and it all revolved around your secret trip to Japan."

"Japan?" Mai-hua said. "Why did you go to—"

I shook my head and held up my palm to silence her. "All in good time, Mei-hua."

Sir Victor looked away from Mei-hua. He looked back at

me. "What does my trip have to do with the murder and the planned kidnapping?"

"Let's be clear on one thing, Sir Victor," I said, trying to answer his question. "There never was an actual attempt to kidnap you. There was, however, a *plot* to kidnap you as you walked out of *Wing On*. This was conceived of for reasons I'll explain in a few minutes.

"The plot failed when you didn't show up at the store, but instead sent your comprador there in your place. That, of course, was because you were in Japan."

Sassoon nodded. I turned to look at Eli and Mei-hua.

"As you both likely know — especially you, Eli — Sir Victor has been a generous and active philanthropist with respect to Jewish charities in Shanghai. He especially has been helpful in terms of the Jewish refugees who have immigrated to Shanghai to escape the Nazis."

"He — I mean, *you* — certainly have been, Sir Victor," Eli said, looking at Sassoon. "We all appreciate your efforts to help our community."

I continued. "It came to your attention, Sir Victor, before your secret trip that the Municipal Council intended to pass a law prohibiting any further immigration of Jewish refugees into the city. In fact, just before you left for Japan, such a bill was submitted to the Council. I understand it currently is undergoing review by a committee."

I looked at Sassoon, and said, "Why don't you tell Mei-hua and Eli the purpose of your trip."

Sir Victor re-lit a cigar, then looked at Eli and Mei-hua.

"My trip had two purposes," Sassoon said.

"First, because the Japanese and Jewish people have had a good, long-standing relationship, I hoped the Imperial government would instruct the three Kwantung-sponsored Japanese members who now sit on the Council to block the pending anti-immigration bill.

"Second, I hoped to obtain a large loan from the Imperial government which I would use to bring more Jewish refugees to Shanghai. I would also use part of the loan to aid Jewish refugees who have already settled in Shanghai. I would especially try to improve their dwelling conditions."

"Were you successful?" Mei-hua said.

Sassoon nodded. "In part. I obtained a loan, although not one as large as I hoped, but I have not been able to block the pending anti-immigration bill. It still is possible the Council will prohibit any additional Jewish immigration into Shanghai."

"Sun-jin just referred to your trip as secret," Eli said. "Why did you keep it secret?"

"I have enemies among several members of the Council. Some of them hate me because I am Jewish; others hate me because they fear me and the power my wealth brings me. Others detest me because I have the ability to foreclose on their sacred Shanghai Club, to bring about its end, because I hold its mortgage.

"If the Council had known in advance of my trip and why I went to Japan, it's likely the immigration bill would have been rushed through the committee and the Council, and would have become law while I was away, defeating the very purpose of my trip."

"That makes sense," Mei-hua said. "But what does that have do with your comprador's murder and with the reason you made Sun-jin investigate a kidnapping you knew had not occurred?"

CHAPTER 65

I LOOKED AT SIR VICTOR, THEN back at Mei-hua. "I'll answer that question," I said. "I'll begin by explaining an aspect of the kidnapping plot that directly ties-in with the question."

Sassoon relit his cigar, and said, "Get on with it, Sun-jin. I don't have all day. I have a business to run here."

I nodded, then looked back at Mei-hua. "*Shi* — *Yes.* As I said a few minutes ago, although Sir Victor was not kidnapped, and, as far as I know, there never was an actual attempt made to kidnap him, there was a kidnapping plan set in motion against him. It just didn't occur because Sir Victor did not show up at *Wing On* where he was expected to be.

"Would you like to know who thought up the kidnapping plan?" I asked.

I paused a few seconds for dramatic effect. It worked. Everyone stared at me.

"The kidnapping plan was conceived of by Chief Inspector Chapman." I paused to give everyone time to react to this news.

"What?" Eli said.

"That son-of-a-bitch," Sassoon said. "I'll have his head."

Mei-hua merely smiled.

"Why?" Eli said.

"Chapman tried to arrange to have Sir Victor kidnapped

to curry favor with members of the Municipal Council," I said, "especially with those members who despise Sir Victor.

"Chapman is an opportunist who sees a plot to fire him from his job under every rock. He lives to be approved by members of the Council.

"How would kidnapping Sir Victor obtain the favor he desires?" Eli said.

"Several ways," I said. "We all know from the newspapers that the Kwantung has been demanding that they automatically have at least five more seats on the Council since the Dwarf Bandits' population is the largest foreign population in Shanghai.

"And we all know that the Council has resisted this, believing that the three existing seats it conceded to the Kwantung last year are sufficient representation for the Dwarf Bandits.

"One of the Council's members suggested to Chapman that if Sir Victor were kidnapped, whether or not he could be rescued, the Council could blame that crime on the Dwarf Bandits, and thereby halt the spread of the Kwantung's influence in our local government.

"The thought was to cause outrage among the non-Japanese population of Shanghai, especially the British and Americans, and thereby slow down or stop the influence of the Dwarf Bandits in the city."

"Nasty bugger, that Chapman," Sassoon said. "I'll deal with him myself."

"It certainly didn't hurt Chapman's cause," I said, "that several members of the Council already hate you, Sir Victor. That played right into the chief inspector's plan."

Sassoon shook his head. His face and neck remained darkened.

"As I said, the plan was foiled when Sir Victor failed to show up to meet with *Wing On*'s president."

"How did Chapman know I was supposed to be there?" Sassoon said.

"Chapman told me, when I met with him yesterday, that he'd put the word out on the street, with the promise of a significant *squeeze* payout, that he was to be kept advised of your schedule or of anything unusual affecting you. Apparently, the chief inspector was informed of the meeting by someone in the *Wing On*'s president's office when the meeting was set up."

"But why murder the comprador if the plan had been to kidnap Sir Victor?" Mei-hua asked.

"Fair question. Before I answer, that, however, I want to talk about how Chapman handled the kidnapping plot that had failed.

CHAPTER 66

"When Chapman's plan to kidnap Sir Victor failed, Chapman still was forced to launch an investigation into the comprador's murder since a major crime had been committed. It just wasn't the crime the chief inspector had counted on.

"Furthermore, to appease Sir Victor's business partners who were concerned that Sir Victor had not been heard from or been found, Chapman quietly initiated an official SMP kidnapping investigation that he knew would go nowhere because, as he alone knew, Sir Victor had not been kidnapped.

"After sufficient time passed without any results from the SMP's kidnapping investigation, Chapman quietly shut it down.

"But Sir Victor's partners were not to be ignored. They raised their concerns again about Sir Victor's well-being and his continued absence from Shanghai. To placate them once more, the chief inspector hired me to act on behalf of the SMP to continue the kidnapping investigation.

"It turns out, Sir Victor," I said, as I looked directly at him, "I was intended by the chief inspector to be nothing more than a strawman for the benefit of your business partners. My role, of course, as far as Chapman was concerned, ended when you reappeared in Shanghai."

Sir Victor stared at me. He was not happy.

"Chapman has no idea who he's dealing with," he said. "I have a long memory."

I paused, then said, "Do you have a question for me, Sir Victor?"

He nodded. "An obvious one you should have already covered. Why was my comprador gunned down?"

"The answer is simple," I said. "Your comprador died because he was loyal to you."

"Explain yourself," Sassoon said.

"What I am about to say is speculation on my part, but speculation founded in logic.

"Neither I nor the chief inspector, who told me he's not had any contact with the kidnappers since that plot failed, really knows the answer to your question. But here is what I believe.

"When your comprador emerged from *Wing On,* the killers expected to see you, Sir Victor, not him. When you thereafter failed to appear, they likely tried to coerce your comprador into telling them where they could find you.

"I assume that when he refused to tell them that you were away from Shanghai, since he knew your trip to Japan was secret, they threatened him. When he still refused to expose information about your trip, they shot him."

"I have a question," Mei-hua said.

"Go on."

"How did you figure out that Chief Inspector Chapman was behind all this?"

CHAPTER 67

"BEFORE I ANSWER THAT, I should say that I don't believe Chapman was behind this alone. I've concluded he was acting on behalf of someone who is a member of the Council, although I have not been able to identify that person.

"Why do I think that?"

I waited for someone to respond, but no one did so I started talking again.

"You should recall that I worked with the chief inspector for many years before I became a PI. I know him well. Chapman is not someone who will initiate actions that might hurt his career. He is not a risk taker, although he can be prodded into taking a risk by someone who is a higher authority than he is, such as a Council member, if not taking that risk might damage his career. He is, as I said, an opportunist.

"In this instance, I believe, Chapman attempted to curry favor with some Council member who hates you, Sir Victor, and, to do so, he plotted the kidnapping to get rid of you.

"I believe your survival or not from that potential ordeal was immaterial to Chapman. Either way, he would have achieved his goal in the eyes of the Council member."

I paused to take a question, but none came.

"I recently met with Chapman and confronted him about this. He would not tell me who was behind this with him, but it's telling that he also did not deny there was someone else involved, someone on the Council. I doubt we'll ever know who that was.

"Now, Mei-hua, to your question. Why did I suspect Chief inspector Chapman? I'll explain that in a minute. I also suspected someone else. I'll explain that, too. First, a little background."

"I began my investigation of the kidnapping by examining the SMP's investigation of the homicide. I hoped my homicide inquiry would yield clues for me to the kidnapping, as well as to the murder, since I knew — or thought I knew at the time — that two crimes had been committed outside *Wing On*. I assumed they were related.

"I looked through the files to see who had a motive to kill Sir Victor's comprador. When I couldn't find a motive at first, I decided that the comprador's murder had not been the primary, intended crime. I decided that Sir Victor's kidnapping was primary. As it turned out, I was correct.

"So, who was it I suspected?" I said.

"At first, after Eli and I met with him, I suspected the comprador's son, Xun Min, of having planned the kidnapping and, perhaps, of having caused the murder of his own father. I theorized that he'd had his father killed so he could step into his father's shoes. I assumed he wanted to succeed his father as Sir Victor's comprador when his father died."

Sir Victor laughed, then turned serious, a scowl on his face. "There was never a chance of that happening," he said, his voice angry.

"That useless son of my comprador was never going to

become my comprador. He was lazy and had none of the skills or experience required for that role. I told his father that several times. I assume his father told him."

"He did tell him. His son told us that when Eli and I met with him.

"In any event," I said, "after meeting with him, I no longer believed that Xun Min arranged to have his father murdered for that or for any other reason.

"As for kidnapping you, Sir Victor, Xun Min would have achieved nothing by participating in that. Plotting against you would not have changed your mind about taking him on as your successor comprador. And, it would have required him to have his father murdered. I didn't see that happening once I'd met him. I ruled out Xun Min as the culprit."

"So, that leaves only Chief Inspector Chapman to be explained," I said. "Let's talk about him."

CHAPTER 68

I HAD EVERYONE'S ATTENTION.

I looked over at Eli. "I began to suspect the chief inspector when you and I, at Sir Victor's insistence, investigated the fake kidnapping."

"Indeed." Sassoon interrupted. I turned my head to face him. "That's exactly why I insisted you pursue that investigation. I wanted to find out who shot my comprador and why they'd done it.

"I looked to you to discover that answer as incidental to your investigation of the fake kidnapping, based on your history of solving difficult crimes. But I never suspected you'd find that Chapman—"

"*Qing — Please!*" I held up my palm to stop him from talking, a gesture that clearly annoyed Sir Victor even more than the fact that I had briefly addressed him in Mandarin, a language I knew he understood from his business dealings in Shanghai.

I looked away from Sassoon, focusing on Eli.

"*Ayeeyah!* I did not expect to learn what I learned, but as our investigation of the fake kidnapping proceeded, I noticed that Chapman often was reluctant to cooperate with me, as if he was worried I might discover something I wasn't supposed to know.

I looked back at Sassoon. "He reminded me often that he had closed down the official SMP investigation of your kidnapping, because the crime had not occurred."

I turned back to face Eli. "That's the reason, I believe, he refused to allow me to bring you into our meeting the one time you came along with me. I realize now he was concerned you might discover something he didn't intend us to know if you sat in when we discussed the fake crime."

"I wondered about that," Eli said.

"I suppose he thought that if I discovered something, he and I could deal with it cop-to-cop if he and I were the only ones who knew about it.

"Once I became suspicious of Chapman's role, things that had not made sense to me before started to make sense. For example, I always wondered why Chapman thought Sir Victor had been kidnapped even though there was no evidence at the murder scene that he had been.

"I now know from my recent conversation with him that Chapman believed the kidnapping at *Wing On* had occurred, as he'd planned, except for the unplanned murder of the comprador. He told me that his belief was reinforced when Sir Victor's business partners came to him because they had not heard from Sir Victor for five weeks.

"I asked him if he had contacted the kidnappers during that five-week period. He told me he tried to reach them several times, but had not been able to contact them. He said he assumed they'd had second thoughts concerning the abduction because of the unplanned homicide, had killed Sir Victor to cover their tracts, and then had fled Shanghai."

I turned directly to face Sassoon. "*Dúi bú qi, Sir Victor — Sorry to say this, Sir Victor.* Chapman confirmed to me that he assumed I would learn of your death when I investigated the abduction for the SMP. He seemed to have taken it for granted that the kidnappers would kill you to cover their tracks."

I watched Sir Victor lean forward in his chair. His eyes were fixed on me. This seemed to be the first time he was fully interested in what I had to say.

"I also suspected Chapman because he frequently instructed me to cease investigating the fake kidnapping, even though Sir Victor insisted I move forward with the investigation. I thought that was strange since the chief inspector, in all my prior experience with him, had always deferred to Sir Victor's wishes. Now he opposed them."

"Good point," Sassoon said.

"I met with Chapman to confront him with all this. When I did, he laughed, told me I was crazy, and then he threatened, as he'd done before, to arrest me for operating without a PI's license and for carrying a pistol for which I had no permit.

"I told him to do just that, to arrest me, that I would use the opportunity to publicly expose him for the crimes I had described to him. When I reminded him that this time I likely would have Sir Victor's assistance in protecting myself, he backed down.

"He then reluctantly conceded my allegations, but said that if I ever disclosed any of this to anyone, he would deny everything. He also said he doubted I could prove any of what I'd said, that it would be the word of a disgraced, former policeman against the word of a decorated chief inspector. *Ayeeyah!* I conceded that point.

"He asked what I wanted, what I expected to achieve from

my allegations against him. I told him I merely wanted his admissions, then, because Sir Victor had not been harmed, I would end the case quietly, just between him and me.

"Chapman had looked skeptical at my statement. He said to me, *And that is all you expect from this? Nothing else?*"

"That's all, Chief Inspector," I said. "I have no other interest in pursuing this." Then I realized there was something I did want.

"There is something I want," I said. "You will promptly reinstate my PI license and will issue me a permit for my pistol."

"Did he do that?" Mei-hua asked.

"*Bú – No.* The chief inspector reminded me that only the Council could do that, that he did not have that power. I agreed and dropped that demand.

"I asked him to tell me the name of the person on the Council who was involved. He refused. He indicated, as I expected he would, that he would never identify that member.

"Finally, he said again that he would deny our conversation if it ever came up. I said it would not come up from me. I then left his office."

I sat back and relaxed. I had no more to offer.

"Well done, Sun-jin," Sassoon said. "You may keep your word with Chapman as far as I'm concerned. Don't bring this up again. I will deal with him in good time, in my own way."

Sir Victor paused. "Plot to kidnap me, will he? I'll see about that."

Mei-hua cleared her throat to grab our attention.

"*Ayeeyah!* You mean the chief inspector will not be punished for his crime? Not even for causing the comprador's murder by setting up the original kidnapping plot? How is that fair? And what about the Council member? Shouldn't he be punished"

"You're right, of course, Mei-hua.," I said. "It's not fair, but it's practical, and would still be the likely outcome even if I were to accuse him.

"The crimes Chapman committed, or that he attempted to commit, all go to intent and motive — his intent or motive or the intent or motive of the Council member who conspired with him.

"As for Chapman, there would be a legal problem if I formally accused him. The burden on the Crown of proving his intent or motive in court would be very high. All the so-called evidence I raised is circumstantial, at best, and, at worst, really is just logical speculation by me.

"This is so even though the chief inspector admitted each matter to me in our meeting. Since he would not make such admissions in court, my conclusions would come across as mere conjecture."

Me-hua frowned and slowly shook her head.

"Also," I said, looking directly at Mei-hua, "I believe the Council would step in to protect Chapman once he made it known — as I expect he would — that he engaged in his unlawful acts to benefit the Council and to benefit Shanghai by blaming the Dwarf Bandits.

"It wouldn't hurt him, either," I added, "to remind them that he acted, as well, to punish Sir Victor."

Everyone was silent as they absorbed this idea. Eli was the first to speak.

"Who tried to kill you, Sun-jin — twice? And why?"

"I don't know. It was likely arranged by Chapman or, perhaps, by the Council member. I think both attacks were meant as warnings to me, to scare me off the case, rather than to kill me. Otherwise, I expect, I would be dead."

"Why did the chief inspector try to stop you from investigating the fake kidnapping?" Eli said.

"For the same reason Sir Victor just said why he wanted me to investigate it. Chapman probably worried I might accidentally discover something that would tie him to the homicide if I continued to pursue the fake crime."

"What about me?" Mei-hua said. "Who tried to kill me?"

"I don't know, but it probably was Chapman. As I told you at the time, I think the attack against you was meant as a warning to me, through you, to have me drop my investigation. Otherwise, you would have been stabbed while you were passed out, lying on the floor."

"*Ayeeyah*," Mei-hua said. "That's some comfort."

CHAPTER 69

THAT EVENING, AT MY FLAT, Mei-hua, Bik, and I celebrated the outcome of the investigations. Mei-hua and I drank *Baijiu*, a Chinese whiskey that is much like the vodka the White Russians in Frenchtown seem to enjoy. Bik gnawed on a water-buffalo bone Mei-hua brought for her.

"We enter a new phase in our lives now that the investigations have ended and Sir Victor considers me a valuable ally for him," I said. "Our lives should now be better in every respect."

"We? Our lives? Tell me why you speak that way?" Mei-hua said.

"Because I am asking you to blend our lives, to become my bride," I said. "That is, if you will be willing to bind yourself to a conservative Confucian. I look forward to seeing you in a beautiful black wedding dress."

Mei-hua laughed and moved over to sit by me.

"Of course I will," she said. "I will gladly be your wife. I will do it for the sake of our four-legged daughter. But I don't know about any wedding dress. I have my reputation as a revolutionary to live up to. One wedding dress could set me back years." She laughed and took my hand.

"And, I might have to re-train you somewhat," she said. "I know that the spirit of Mao dwells within you, somewhere, if you only will admit it to yourself and stop resisting his teachings."

I frowned and became rigid.

Mei-hua squeezed my hand. "I'm only kidding you," she said. "In fact, Eli and I spoke recently about this. We agreed that you've been correct.

"It is too dangerous for us to continue to work for the CCP. We have too many suspicious eyes watching us, eyes that belong to dangerous men such as Tu and Harue. We have decided to retire from all Party activities."

I smiled, until she said, "That is, until the war has ended, and China has emerged victorious over the Dwarf Bandits."

As we hugged, then kissed, Bik dropped to the floor from the window sill, walked over to us, and growled.

I looked at her, thinking she was jealous. I was ready to bend over to pet her, but that was not it.

Bik turned away from us and walked back to the window. She put her front paws on the window sill, and looked down at the street. She growled again.

Mei-hua and I walked over to look.

The street was filled with Kwantung tanks, more than I've seen on other occasions when its troops marched in lines four abreast.

"I wonder what's going on?" Mei-hua said. "The troops are waving Japan's flag and singing as they march. I've never seen them do that before."

"The large number of troops and tanks in the parade also seems strange," I said.

"I'll turn on the radio. Maybe we can get some information.

When my Emerson warmed up, the words of the announcer were chilling.

. . . And so, ladies and gentlemen of Shanghai, I repeat the only information we have so far.

Earlier this morning, at approximately 7:00 a.m., on this December 8, 1941, the armed forces of Japan attacked Pearl Harbor, in the Hawaiian Islands, a territory held by the United States of America.

Shortly thereafter, the armed forces of Japan attacked the Philippine Islands, Wake Island, and British Malaya.

A state of war now exists between Japan and the United States as well as between Japan and Great Britain.

Here in Shanghai, troops of the Japanese Imperial Army stationed in the city's outlying districts have invaded the International Settlement held by Great Britain and the United States. The Kwantung, out of respect for Japan's ally, Vichy France, has not marched into the French Concession.

Shanghai now is fully occupied by the Kwantung.

There will be more to come as we learn

> more. Keep your radios turned on for more information.
>
> This is Station KLDM, Radio Shanghai, signing off until we have more information for you.

"This is not good," I said. "Not good at all."

"What do you think this will mean for us?"

I shrugged, glanced out the window at the Kwantung below, and said, "We will have to keep a low profile, stay out of trouble with the Dwarf Bandits, and try to avoid being shipped to an internment camp. All as I try to earn a living as a PI."

I put my arm around Mei-hua's shoulder and pulled her in close to me. She kissed my cheek and leaned her head on my shoulder.

Bik continued to stare out the window at the troops below.

THE END

PLEASE REVIEW *SLEEPING WITH THE TIGER* ON AMAZON

If you enjoyed ***SLEEPING WITH THE TIGER***, please post a review on Amazon at **www.Amazon.com**. Search for the book review page under my name or under the book's title, ***SLEEPING WITH THE TIGER***.

DOWNLOAD A FREE COPY *MANDARIN YELLOW*

The first Socrates Cheng mystery

Copy and paste this link into your browser or, if you are reading the page on a tablet or other digital device, click this link to download a free copy: http://www.stevenmroth.com/FreeBook.aspx

Visit me at www.StevenMRoth.com to see all of my published books and receive information about my upcoming books

ACKNOWLEDGEMENTS

First, of course, my thanks to Dominica who, as always, both encouraged me to write, and then supported my efforts.

I am fortunate to have had several people who acted as my early reading team — reading the manuscript before it was finalized, and tearing into several parts of it, forcing me to re-think several scenes and chapters. You all improved my book. Since some of you have expressed your desire to remain anonymous, I won't name anyone, but you know who you are, and you have my gratitude.

BIOGRAPHY

Steve has written (i) a three-book mystery series featuring his Chinese/Greek/American private eye — Socrates Cheng, (ii) a two-book thriller/suspense series featuring ex-Navy SEAL Trace Austin, and (iii) a two-book mystery series that takes place in Shanghai, China in the 1930s and 1940s. SLEEPING WITH THE TIGER is the third book in the Shanghai mystery series.

Steve holds a bachelor's degree in philosophy and history from Pennsylvania State University and a law degree from Duke Law School. He is retired from law practice and lives with his wife in Washington, DC.

Visit Steve's web site for more information about his books: www.stevenmroth.com

Made in the USA
Monee, IL
15 April 2021

65799382R10169